The FIVE LIVES *of* OUR CAT ZOOK

AMULET BOOKS
NEW YORK

The Five Lives of our Cat Zook

JOANNE ROCKLIN

AUTHOR'S NOTE

"Miraculo and the Twenty-Six Toes" is an original story by the author, as far as she knows. As is "Mud."

The "ghost story" section of "Jewel the Ghost Cat" is derived from similar folktales from around the world, using the motif, or theme, of "A Corpse Claims Its Property." (Source: Aarne-Thompson-Uther type 366, translated and edited by D. L Ashliman, 2000–2008; http://www.pitt.edu/~dash/type0366.html).

"Beau the Flying Cat" is also a variant of folktales from many countries, using the motif "The Talkative Tortoise." (Source: Aarne-Thompson-Uther type 225A, edited by D. L. Ashliman, 1999–2010; http://www.pitt.edu/~dash/type0225a.html).

Library of Congress Cataloging-in-Publication Data

Rocklin, Joanne.
The five lives of our cat Zook / by Joanne Rocklin.
p. cm.
ISBN 978-1-4197-0192-4
[1. Cats—Fiction. 2. Brothers and sisters—Fiction.] I. Title.
PZ7.R59Fi 2012
[Fic]—dc23
2011041088

Book design by Maria T. Middleton

Printed and bound in U.S.A.
10 9 8 7 6 5 4

115 West 18th Street
New York, NY 10011
www.abramsbooks.com

for
MY FATHER

The
FIVE LIVES
of
OUR CAT ZOOK

* 1 *

THE IMPORTANT STUFF

Our cat's named Zucchini, and we call him Zook, but that's not the most important thing about him. And neither is the INCREDIBLE fact that he's got seven toes on each front foot and six on each one in the back, for a total of twenty-six. (Most cats have five and four, for a total of eighteen.) His eyes are blue, like old faded jeans, and his coat is dark brown. But when he's lying on a sidewalk scratching his back, you can see some white markings shaped like the state of California on his belly. And some black tufts in the spot where Oakland is, which is where we live. One corner of one ear is clipped off. He's got shaky teeth, black gums, and breath that smells like the restroom in the Chevron station—a smell we love, because it's Zook's.

If you run your palm along his right side, you can feel something like a little pebble stuck under his skin. It's not a pebble. It's a pellet from a BB gun. And that's not the most important thing about him, either. In fact, I try not to think about that so much.

Two and a half years ago, my brother, Fred, and I found Zook in the alley that connects the back of our apartment building with the back of O'Leary's Pizzeria. We go to O'Leary's a lot because of their famous fried zucchini. (Fried is the only kind of vegetable Freddy will eat.)

It was a warm, sunny Saturday, just like this one. Mom was in the stuffy basement laundry room, and Fred and I were sitting out in the alley eating lunch from O'Leary's. We had folding chairs out there, and back then the big blue pots were filled with lavender and red geraniums. You could smell the eucalyptus tree and lavender over the traffic smells. Birds were chirping, which I suppose they're always doing, but this was the kind of day when nice things like that got your attention.

Then something else got our attention.

"EE-OW! EE-OWEY!"

That's another thing about Zook: He's got the greatest pair

of cat lungs ever. There he was, stretched out in the warm dirt of one of those geranium pots, howling away as if he and the birds in the alley were singers in a band. Nowadays, Zook is famous in the neighborhood for his singing, but at the time we'd never heard anything like him before. And then he let Freddy and me pet him, rubbing his head against our legs. Probably hadn't been stroked in a long, long time. I noticed he was wearing a collar with a silver rectangle dangling from it. INCREDIBLY, in the middle of that rectangle was a little sparkly diamond! We lured that starving cat into the building with some fried zucchini. (Get it? Zucchini . . . Zook.) Mom said we could keep him, so we cleaned him up, bought him some cat food, and brought him upstairs to live with us. Dad said our family could always use a diamond, or the gobs of cash you could get for it.

That diamond isn't even the most important thing about him. Anyway, we found out it was fake. But we'd already started to love Zook by the time we absolutely found out for sure. Actually, I began to love him the second I met him.

The most important thing about Zook right now is that he's sick, and Fred and I are waiting around on the steps of the Good Samaritan Veterinary Clinic, where Zook's getting help. The clinic has big windows in the front, and Freddy keeps jumping up to look in.

"There he is! I see him!" Fred shouts.

I push myself up from the stone stairs. I feel like a tired old lady, even though I'm only ten.

"Where?" I say. I don't see Zook anywhere.

It's Saturday, so the office is busy. A woman is answering the phone at the front desk, a man is bending over a filing cabinet, people and their pets are sitting around on couches, and a man with a stethoscope in his shirt pocket is scratching a slobbery golden retriever's ear while talking to its owner.

"There!" Fred says, and I realize he isn't talking about Zook. Fred's pointing to the stethoscope guy. "That's Zook's vet!"

"Oh, yeah," I say. It was kind of a blur when my mom and Fred and me rushed Zook in that morning, but that's the guy.

Fred is looking at him like he's God or something. Just like a five-year-old, to think like that. Of course, it is sort of godlike to cure a living, breathing being. Then a really SCARY question pops into my head. Even though Zook's vet is probably a good person who loves animals with all his heart, does that also mean he's good at his job? I mean really, really good?

We go inside and stand near the vet's elbow. He's explaining to the slobbery golden's owner that the dog's medicine has to be given three times a day for the first three days, then two times a day for the next three days, then once a day until all the pills are used up.

"I'm sorry. Can you repeat that one more time?" says the golden's owner, a man who looks just as smart as you or me, except for the fact that his sweater is on inside out.

The vet takes a breath, holds up the little bottle of pills, and explains again, in a fake-patient voice, about the three times a day for the first three days, etc., etc. Fake-patient voices are always easy to spot because of the slowed-down syllables.

"Hope I remember all that," says the dog's owner.

I can hear unhappy yipping coming from behind the big closed doors past the front desk, and you can't miss Zook's famous yowling over it all: "EE-OW! EE-OWEY!" Yes, there's lots of stuff for the vet to do back there, like take care of Zook, for instance! And when we brought Zook into the Good Samaritan Veterinary Clinic, he didn't look one-seventeenth as frisky and healthy as that slobbery golden, who is now happily licking Freddy's shoe.

That's when, all of a sudden, I notice two things. Two important things that make me open my mouth. My big mouth, as some people (OK, my mother) would say.

Gramma Dee says I have *chutzpah*, which is a Yiddish word for "nerve," but I only have it when the situation is serious. Which this is.

The first important thing: The instructions are right there on the pill bottle. IN CAPS.

I think it's important to notice how words are written. *Italics* tell you to emphasize the words, or that the words are new or unusual, or that someone is thinking or writing or singing the words. Quotation marks tell you when someone is talking, or that the speaker is wriggling her fingers as she says a word in order to make that word "special."

It's as if the words have feelings. They come alive!

CAPS are like neon signs, or shouts, and they're even more important than italics. You're REALLY supposed to pay attention to them.

"The instructions are right there on the pill bottle," I say.

The man and Zook's vet both turn to look at me. Then the

dog owner looks down at the caps on the pill bottle. The vet taps his index finger on the bottle—or, more specifically, THE VERY LONG FINGERNAIL ON THE INDEX FINGER OF HIS RIGHT HAND.

You may have guessed that the second important detail I'm noticing is the very long fingernail. Actually, all five of the very long fingernails on his right hand, which could only mean that:

1. Zook's vet is a serious guitar player. And I know exactly what that means, because my friend Riya's uncle is one.
2. Zook's vet wishes he were home, practicing his guitar or playing with his band. Zook's vet and his band want to leave Oakland and go to L.A. to get famous. (That's what Riya's uncle wants to do with his band.)
3. Zook's vet is also thinking about the chords to a new song about his love. Many guitarists—Riya's uncle, for example—sing songs about their loves, haven't you noticed? Zook's vet is thinking about all the words that rhyme with "pretty," like "city" and "witty" and lots of others. He's thinking that nothing rhymes with "beautiful," and it's driving him crazy. Also, should the song be sad and slow, or happy and dancey?

In other words, he's worrying and thinking about all those things. And he's NOT worrying and thinking about ZOOK!

"Excuse me, young lady," says the vet in his fake-patient voice. "Take a seat and I'll be with you as soon as I can."

Freddy and I don't take a seat. I draw myself up tall. I try to put on a serious face, like my mother does when she's putting unkind people in their place. I say what she would say in this situation.

"I beg your pardon," I say, even though I'm not really begging his pardon, and tears are showing up in my eyes, which wouldn't happen to my mother.

Freddy says, "We want to know about Zook, please!"

Fred is still looking all googly-eyed at the vet, like he's God. Fred actually looks at a lot of adults like that, especially father-figure types. But God would remember who Zook is. I can tell by the way the vet pauses and studies the ceiling, like something important is going on up there, that the vet doesn't have a CLUE. Of course, the vet's memory is poor today, after a late night out playing a gig with his band, showing off for his love with fancy guitar strumming.

Then I give the vet a clue. Lots of them.

"I'm Oona Armstrong, and this is my brother, Fred," I say. "Don't you remember us? We just brought in our cat this morning! Zook's the big old brown cat, with faded blue eyes, with a clipped ear, and the state of California on his belly. He has bad teeth and gums, but that's not the problem. He has a BB-gun pellet on his right flank, but that's not the problem, either. We brought him in this morning because the problem is—the problems ARE—he's stopped eating and he keeps staring into space, and when he isn't staring into space, he's hiding in dark places, or staring into his water bowl, too tired to drink."

The golden retriever's owner gives a kind of salute to Zook's vet and leaves. And now Zook's vet really looks at us. I can tell he remembers our cat because of all the clues I gave him. I guess he feels sorry for us, too, because he takes us down a hall to a door with a window. We're both allowed a quick peek, and there's Zook, a sad brown blob in a cage, a tube hooked up to his paw, and a blue bandage keeping it in place.

"Zook's kidneys are failing, and he's very dehydrated," the vet says. "We're giving him fluids intravenously so he'll feel better. We'll call you when we're done with the treatment. There's nothing you can do now except go home."

I don't like being told there's nothing I can do. I don't like feeling that way, either.

The vet hands me his card, and his name is Howard Fiske, DVM. And there's that long fingernail again! I'm scared for Zook's failing kidneys, so the tears roll out of my eyes, and then a whole lot of really loud caps roll out of my mouth. "WELL, YOU GOTTA MAKE SURE THOSE KIDNEYS PASS, PLEASE!" I say. Loudly.

✶ 2 ✶

THE CATS-HAVE-NINE-LIVES THEORY

So now I'm thinking that wasn't very smart.

"You yelled at Zook's doctor," Fred says on our way home. He's crying, wiping his nose on his sleeve.

"I know, I know," I say. "Hey, don't worry. Nothing's wrong. Zook will get fixed." I feel shivery inside, and I'm crying, too. I'm not sure I believe what I just said.

The vet had patted me on the shoulder and said he understood. But, as I said, that vet isn't God. He's just a plain old human, who eats and sleeps and scratches an itch, like everyone else. A human who really doesn't like being yelled at, and who may not do his very, very best work when he sees Zook. Because when he sees Zook, he will think about Zook's owner with her big mouth and feel super annoyed.

We sit down on our special bus bench, even though we're not waiting for a bus. This particular bench is about halfway between the Good Samaritan Veterinary Clinic and our apartment building on Telegraph Avenue. It's a good place to stop and hang out if you're not in any particular hurry. Also, it's right across the street from a Bank of the West. If there happens to be a bank robbery, I am in the best position to notice important details to help the authorities. For instance, what the bad guys look like when they race outside, the license plate number of the getaway car, the exact time of the event, any witnesses, etc., etc. I'm a good noticer. Not that I've ever witnessed a robbery, but you never know.

I look over at Fred. I notice some important details. He's got that Sad Fred Look, all droopy-mouthed, and I know he'll be eating air again at the next meal. That's what my mom always says, that Fred eats air—boiled, fried, roasted, and grilled. In other words, his appetite isn't so hot. And we're always so scared that he'll go back to that time when he was REALLY wasting away, after our father died, two years ago.

Then I know what to do. It's one of my four jobs. Yes, believe it or not, I have four jobs.

One of my jobs is to crank up Fred's appetite. I reach into the pocket of my shorts and pull out a little plastic bag filled with tiny crackers. Fred likes food that's shaped like cute things. These crackers are shaped like goldfish.

My second job is helping Fred improve his reading skills. I want him to be a STAR when he gets to kindergarten next year. That's what happened to me. Also, reading will take his mind off things and make him happier. And I'm happy when Fred is happy.

I pull out a pencil stub and a little pad from my pocket, handy just for this purpose. I get inspired and draw a really good rebus, if I do say so myself. Rebuses taught me to read and now they're teaching Fred. My dad, the Great Rebus-Maker himself, was the one who taught me.

"*Cats*," reads Fred.

"You got it. Go on."

"*H-h-h-a-a-ve*."

"Great!"

"*Nine. Hives. Cats. Have. Nine. Hives.* They do?"

I point to the code *RW* above my drawing of the hives. "*Rhymes with*, remember? Make *hives* rhyme with something that starts with *L*."

"*L-l-l-ives. Cats have nine lives.*"

"There." I scribble *I* ♥ *Fred* under my rebus.

I feel like Miss Crackenhower must have felt. Miss Crackenhower was my first-grade teacher, way back. Practically everything she ever said was in caps. Her teeth were very white and it looked like she had more of them than a usual human. She was always smiling. That's because you get a happy feeling helping someone read. You feel sort of like a wizard. I have to say, to this day, Miss Crackenhower still has the whitest teeth. And she still seems much happier than any other teacher, especially my fourth-grade teacher, Mr. Fry, who has trouble keeping the lid on Room 7.

"Ha, ha, that's silly! Nine lives!" says Fred, and he gives me a little punch on my arm. Of course he doesn't believe me. And all of a sudden, it's important, VERY important, that Fred understand and believe. He'll feel happier right away. And like I said, I'm happy when Fred is happy.

So I start talking very fast. "Listen to me, Freddy. Cats are born with nine lives inside of them. They have the ability—the POWER—to live nine whole lives! Some of those lives can be very long, and maybe some are shorter, but this is how it works: Whenever something bad happens, like a cat fight, or a bad fall, or a failing kidney, just like that, PRESTO! That cat's back in business again!"

"You mean he dies and comes back again?"

"He sort of dies, but not really. He starts a whole new life. Nine lives altogether. Cats are amazing that way."

The Cats-Have-Nine-Lives Theory is what people call "an old wives' tale." It's a theory that's been around since olden times. Everyone who knows cats knows how often they do dumb, death-defying stunts that would kill other living things. How many cats have you noticed snoozing peacefully under a car? Ever seen a dog do that? I rest my case.

I look around and notice an older woman approaching our bench.

"See her? I'm going to prove it to you," I say quietly out of the corner of my mouth, because the woman is coming closer. Sometimes older people have hearing problems, but sometimes they don't. For instance, Gramma Dee claims she can hear a fly's little hairy legs touching down onto her kitchen countertop.

Now the woman sits down on the bench with us. Fred and I squiggle to the side to make more room.

"But, really, how do you know it's true?" Fred asks, continuing the conversation.

"I just know," I say. "It's one of those things you learn when you get older."

I can feel the woman beside me listening. She smells like mint tea and just-washed laundry. Of course, she can't help listening, since we're all squished together on the bench. But often older people do eavesdrop on kids' conversations, and even jump right in. That's because they miss the children they used to have, who have all grown up and left home.

I smile at her. "Nice day," I say.

I try to keep a couple of good conversation starters up my sleeve. And it's usually a nice day in Oakland, except for a couple of months in the winter when it rains. We even love the rain, especially when there's a drought. But even when there's lots of rain, we all still try to practice water conservation whenever we can. For example, not running the water while we brush our teeth.

"Yes, it sure is a pretty day today," the woman says.

"My brother and I are talking about cats. How many lives would you say they have?" I ask, hoping she'll say the right thing.

"Nine, of course."

BINGO!

"And you wouldn't believe the scrapes my cats have bounced back from!" the woman says. The bus arrives before she can tell us about those scrapes. She waves from a window of the bus, and we wave back.

"See?" I say to Fred. "Just ask anyone."

3

MY RAINBOW WHOPPER THEORY

Here are some things about me:

I am a ten-year-old girl. I like to dip my french fries in vinegar. I love when the sun shines through spiderwebs. My best friend is Riya. I love my little brother so much, my heart hurts. I like dancing and drawing.

I am easily spotted in a crowd because I'm the girl wearing the black Oakland Raiders sweatshirt that's way too big for her because it used to belong to her dad. I pulled it out of a box of old clothes on its way to Goodwill a few months ago. Everywhere I go, people usually yell out "Go Raiders!" I'm not that up on football, but "Go Raiders" can often be a good conversation starter for other topics.

Also, I need to wear glasses, but I am a good noticer, as I

mentioned. Being a noticer helps you come up with inventions and theories and stories. For instance, I noticed that people use a drinking straw only once and then they throw it away. Very wasteful. So one day I invented the Family Straw. Everyone has their own straw permanently attached to a bigger one which would be hooked up to the pitcher of juice or beverage of the family's choice. An excellent water-saving idea, because you wouldn't have to wash all those drinking glasses. And good for the environment because it's just one big straw that you don't have to throw away. I'm still working out the details on how to build it, the materials needed, etc., etc.

My dad used to tell me I have an inventive mind, but I actually prefer thinking up theories and stories rather than inventions. You don't have to build theories and stories, just make them up.

For instance, my Rainbow Whopper Theory.

That's another important thing about me, and I have to admit it, even though it doesn't sound so great. I tell whoppers. Whoppers are lies, plain and simple. Some whoppers are worse than other whoppers, and those are nothing to be proud of. But some whoppers are stories. Those are the good kind. Thinking about different kinds of whoppers can get very complicated and make your brain jump around in your skull, so it helps if you attach colors to them. That's where my Rainbow Whopper Theory comes in.

BLUE whoppers save your scaredy skin, or someone else's, to smooth things over for a while. When I told Mom that Fred didn't flush the goldfish down the toilet (he wanted it to join other fish in the ocean), that was a blue whopper. I told her I did it myself, accidentally.

RED whoppers are the kind that make other people think you're greater than you are. For a long time (OK, up until a year ago), I enjoyed telling everyone that Neil Armstrong, the first man to bounce around on the moon, was my father's second cousin. It just seemed very cool to be related to him.

BLACK whoppers have only one purpose: They are meant to hurt someone. I don't think I've ever told one of these during my lifetime. WHITE ones do the opposite—they make someone feel better. For instance when I was in second grade, I told Sam that, no, he didn't smell like pee like everyone said. Telling someone that cats have nine lives (when you've just made your cat's vet angry) is half blue, half white. Sky blue, maybe.

But then there are the whoppers you don't tell. The kind

when you leave something out and keep the secret all to yourself. Those whoppers are YELLOW.

Here's the thing: When we found Zook lying in that geranium pot in the alley on that sunny Saturday two and a half years ago, something else was attached to his collar besides that rectangle with the fake diamond on it. There was also a name tag. The name tag said *MUD, 1235 Clover Street*, which is around the block from where we live. Here are the reasons I threw that name tag away and never told a living soul about it:

1. I wanted us to keep that cat as our own pet. We renamed him Zook right away. So it was just convenient (blue whopper) to say he was homeless.
2. Zook wanted to stay with us, too! He followed us up to our apartment without a backward glance, as if he knew it was his home. And it was.
3. Only a dork calls their own cat "Mud," and only someone worse than a dork doesn't feed their cat properly, or give him flea medicine, or uses him for target practice with a BB gun!!!!!! A villain does all that. No way was that cat going back to 1235 Clover Street.

I committed that address to memory so I could visit the Villain myself and seek revenge. Not that I had any plans for revenge. Two and a half years ago I wasn't even allowed to go around the block by myself.

But now I'm allowed to go lots of places. I pick up Fred from preschool, and I go to Safeway to buy milk and fruit and stuff, and then there's O'Leary's Pizzeria, where we hang out a lot because of our job (more about that soon), and the Good Samaritan Veterinary Clinic, and the Bank of the West that I investigate in case of robberies. Man, the places I'll get to go when I can drive a car! Six long, long years away, even though my mother and Gramma Dee say it's not anywhere near long enough for them.

Lately, we've been passing by the Villain's house.

Today after leaving the bus stop, we actually do more than pass by. We sit on the curb across from the Villain's house to rest. That's what Fred thinks we're doing, anyway. I myself am noticing things.

Zook's old home is a small house with shades pulled all the way down and a broken-down front porch. Overgrown lavender plants in the yard sweeten up the air, almost completely covering up the chipped front walk. Sometimes I see a motorcycle parked in the sloped gravel driveway, but we've never seen the Villain.

Fred reaches into his little plastic bag for a fish cracker, his mind still on my whopper.

"How many lives has Zook lived already?" he asks.

"Nobody knows for sure. But trust me, less than nine."

Right now I feel like grabbing a sharp pebble, then racing across the street to scratch a big *Z* for Zook on the shiny hub of that motorcycle's front wheel.

"But how many do you think?" Fred asks.

I brush a crumb from his chin. I look right into his worried brown eyes. "Zook is working on his fifth life," I say, pulling a number out of the air. Well, not exactly out of the air, because five is Fred's favorite number, being a proud five-year-old himself.

Fred nods thoughtfully, then counts on his fingers. "Four left."

He eats a bunch of crackers and his mouth is stuffed when he asks the next question. It comes out sounding like "How shoe your snow?" or "Cows moo and blow?" But I'm prepared for the question, so I understand him perfectly.

"How do I know? I'll tell you how I know," I say. "Cats give us 'clues,' that's what they do. If you're a real good noticer, you pick up those clues, those really important details. Those clues tell you about all the lives before, and maybe even all the lives coming up."

"Oh," says Fred, in a way that means there will be more questions later. "OK. Anyway, let's go now." He doesn't look worried anymore, and stands up.

I hear a jingle of keys. There he is! The Villain, double-locking his front door. And sure enough, he looks like a pirate. I've never actually seen a pirate personally, except in drawings. But I can imagine a pirate like the Villain, handsome and brown-skinned, with a black braid down his back and a red shirt with yellow fringes on it. A pirate wouldn't be holding a motorcycle helmet, but you get the picture.

The Villain waves at us. "Hey," he says.

"I heart your bike!" says Freddy.

The Villain grins, flashing his white pirate teeth. "Come over and take a look!"

His smile looks evil. OK, to be fair, his smile would be an ordinary one on anyone else. But knowing what I know about his BB-gun activities, it looks evil to me. I narrow my eyes at him. I once saw a cop do that on TV.

"Let's go," I say to Freddy, grabbing his arm.

"Aw, I wanna touch his bike!" Freddy says.

Freddy is young. He doesn't understand things about the world. He doesn't understand about the evil that lurks in some people's hearts. Riya and I talk about that all the time. You just never know, which is why I wasn't allowed to go around the block by myself until I was old enough to know certain things. You just don't make friends with everyone you meet, people who look perfectly fine, but could very well have hearts oozing with evil. At ten, I've figured out the difference between a pirate who shoots at cats and a lady at a bus stop who smells like mint tea.

"No," I say firmly. The Villain shrugs. He and his braid roar off on that motorcycle, and Freddy and I head to O'Leary's.

4

MY THIRD AND FOURTH JOBS

When we walk into O'Leary's Pizzeria, Fred asks everyone about the Cats-Have-Nine-Lives Theory. He asks Manic Moe the dough-maker and dough-tosser, Salvatore the dishwasher, and Vicki the server. He asks most of the Saturday lunch crowd, whose names I don't know. He also asks My Secret Love, hunched over his cell phone, eating a double slice. (*His* name I know, but I'm not saying.) And because Fred is little and cute, they don't think he's crazy when he asks his question. They all give the right answer, too: nine.

Except for Mario and Maria, the owners. By the way, nobody knows who O'Leary was, but Mario and Maria have no plans to change the sign. Mario was born in Italy and Maria was born in Mexico. People are curious about Irish pizza, and then they come in and eat the best Italian or Mexican pizza of their lives. Not to mention the famous fried zucchini. The Mexican-style pizza comes with an optional topping of crazy-hot chilis—"Only for the brave of heart and stomach," according to a sign on the wall.

"I say seven," says Mario. "Seven lives."

And I say, "What do you mean, seven?" I toss my head in Fred's direction and wiggle my nose nine times to get Mario to play along.

But Mario doesn't notice. "Seven. We even have a saying in Italy. *I gatti hanno sette vite.* Cats have seven lives. RIGHT, MARIA?" Mario shouts to his wife, who is in the back room.

"WHAT?" she shouts back.

"CATS HAVE SEVEN LIVES!"

Maria pokes her head out, sees me and Fred, and waves. "That's what they say in Italy," she says. "In Mexico, I've heard it's eight and a half."

"Well," I say, "Zook lives in the United States. Here, cats have nine."

Mario serves us one Daily Slice each, which is always the same, served every day: three-cheese with parsley flecks and fried zook. Fred picks off the parsley because it's green.

"What have you got against green?" we always ask. Fred never knows. You would think brown food or fuchsia food or blue food would be a no-no if the color of food was important to you. Things people like and don't like don't always make sense—ever notice? Vicki brings us some extra zucchini. Of course zucchini is also green, but these are covered in batter, then fried. Fred doesn't eat much of his pizza, but he does eat the zucchini because covered-up green is OK, according to him.

We get free food and are treated well at O'Leary's Pizzeria because Fred and I, we're employees of this establishment. Our job is dressing up in a cardboard triangle of pizza and a little pointed hat (me) and a brown cardboard zucchini circle (Fred). Fred might look like an olive if you didn't know about O'Leary's famous fried zucchini, but that doesn't really matter. Both of our cardboards say O'LEARY'S PIZZERIA on them. We're supposed to dance around to attract business right outside the door so the other O'Leary's employees can see us.

It's a good feeling to walk in and hear Mario shout, "Hey, serve these kids anything they want! Anything at all! They are employees of this establishment!"

Of course, there's not much you can choose from except

pizza and fried zook, but who cares? We love our job. Mario and Maria used to serve us teeny cups of espresso with lots of milk and sugar in it, but my mother put a stop to that. They also used to pay us two dollars each per week, but my mother put a stop to that, too. She said Mario and Maria didn't need to pay us for doing something that was fun. Does that make sense? Lots of people get paid for doing something fun! Circus workers and astronauts, for instance. I even offered to contribute most of it to household expenses, because my mom has a furlough from her job at Sears, which means her hours were cut back.

"We're not in dire straits yet," my mother said. "Payment with pizza is good enough."

When we finish our pizza, we start working. Maria hands us a boom box and some water bottles. Then out the door we go.

We turn up the music real loud. Today Maria and Mario have chosen the Rolling Stones for their future customers' listening pleasure.

Then Freddy and I dance. Well, I dance. Fred jumps around a lot and kicks his little legs out in front of him.

"Don't forget to point," I remind him, because that's the

real reason for our job. We are supposed to point up at the big O'Leary's Pizzeria sign on top of the restaurant to remind people that a slice would really hit the spot right about now.

It's hard to remember to point when you're dancing, but we are doing our best.

People wave at us from cars and honk their horns. We wave back. A young man goes into O'Leary's, probably because of Freddy and me. And all of a sudden I realize I haven't thought about Zook in a while. It's hard to be worried and sad when you're dancing and doing a favor for good friends.

My Secret Love comes out. I call his name. He pulls the earplugs from his ears and raises his eyebrows.

"IT'S ME! OONA!" I shout above the music of the boom box. I want to really make sure he remembers my name. I take off my little pointed hat in case he doesn't recognize me.

"Oh, hi," he says. "I'm not used to talking to a slice of pizza, but, hey, why not?"

Why not! That is SO wise. So many things would be possible in this world if you thought *Why not?* all day long.

"NICE DAY, HUH?" I shout. I am hoping he'll walk over and continue our conversation.

"Sure is. Have a good one!" he says, and keeps on walking.

Maybe "Nice day" isn't the greatest conversation starter because it can lead to "Have a good one," which is pretty much a conversation ender. I really don't know how to talk to a boy in junior high who has his own smartphone.

I watch My Secret Love stroll away. I'm still holding my little pointed hat in front of me. A woman walking by stops and says, "Maybe this will help a bit, dear." Then she drops a five-dollar bill into my hat!

Right after that, *plink! plink!* A man drops in two quarters. Fred is still jumping and pointing and doesn't notice. He's young. Five-year-olds mostly notice what's close up to their noses. Experienced noticers notice the details as well as the big picture. I lean my hat against the boom box just to see what will happen, and I start dancing again. Next thing you know, my hat is halfway filled up with coins and a couple of bills. Soon Fred notices the money and stops dancing.

"Wow," he says.

"Let's take a break," I say.

We take all our stuff and go to the back alley that connects O'Leary's with our apartment building. The O'Leary's kitchen opens to the alley, and when Salvatore sees us sitting there, he gets us another plate of zook to share.

Freddy and I love this alley, and not only because we found Zook here that sunny Saturday, singing his heart out in a pot of geraniums. One of my dreams in life is to have a real backyard, and this alley is a good substitute, even though it's all concrete. When I take off my glasses to wipe them on my sweatshirt, things look even prettier, in a dreamy sort of way. The branches from a backyard camellia tree hang over the fence, so part of the alley is always shady and cool. Other spots are sunny and great for growing things in pots.

Like I said before, there used to be lavender and geraniums out here in big blue pots. My dad had planted them. He also planted yarrow and catmint in the wide cracks of the concrete for the stray cats to enjoy. He had big plans to put pink paving stones on top of the concrete. Big plans. But then life got in the way. Now yellow and purple flowers are bursting through those cracks, and it's almost as nice as having pavers.

Of course, it used to be much prettier back here when the big blue pots had lavender plants and geraniums in them. They all dried up, so someone threw them away. There's only dirt in there now. Maybe the plants would have grown back if they'd had a chance. We could plant more, but my mom says we would need to buy fresh soil and fertilizer and water them regularly, which is hard to remember to do when life gets in the way. I clean out the cigarette butts every now and then.

My mom and dad and Maria and Mario and I used to hang out here a lot. Freddy was little then, sitting on my mother's lap. Freddy doesn't really remember those times, not even the day we found Zook. But I tell him all about those special times, so he thinks he remembers. That's why he loves it back here as much as I do.

Anyway, cats still love it back here, too, because of that catmint, just like my dad said they would. Of course, they also like the mice at night and the O'Leary's trash bins. The alley smells of cat pee, but we don't mind. Cat pee isn't a bad smell if you have a cat that you love.

We lean our cardboard costumes against the wall, where someone has painted Elvis Lives in giant blue and red caps. Elvis Presley was a rock-and-roll star who died a long time ago. I've seen him on YouTube. Some people are convinced Elvis Presley is still alive, roaming around somewhere. They love him so much, they just can't bear to say good-bye, my gramma tells us. Gramma Dee herself used to scream with joy when she heard him sing his famous songs about blue suede shoes and hound dogs. Riya thinks those are weird topics to sing about. But Riya has never had a pet she's loved with all her heart.

"Elvis lives!" reads Freddy.

Freddy is so proud that he can read that all by himself, without a "rhymes with" or any other help from me. We sit down, leaning against the wall, me against the *E*, Fred against the *L*. We take long drinks from our water bottles. Then I pour all the money out of my hat. Ten quarters, eight dimes, three one-dollar bills, and the five-dollar bill that started it all.

"Eleven dollars and thirty cents," I say. I want to keep the money so much, even though I got it with the help of a yellow whopper. It just feels so good to have extra money in your pocket—ever notice?

"That's a lot of money," says Freddy.

"Let's keep it a secret awhile, OK?" I say. "Promise?" I hunch over the money and turn my back so Salvatore and Manic Moe can't see it.

"Sure, I promise," Freddy says. "I love secrets!"

Then Fred asks a question I had a feeling he'd ask sooner or later. Except I guess I thought it would be later.

"Oona, how many lives do human beans have?"

"Only one. But don't worry. It's a long, long one."

My heart hurts, because that's a whopper, too. A white one, but a big one for sure. Our dad did not have a long life. He died of cancer when he was thirty-one. Freddy blinks like he knows I've told a lie, but the dots aren't all connected for him yet.

And now I don't feel like hearing more questions from Freddy. I just feel like telling him other whoppers, so he'll feel better. Before he connects the dots and thinks about our dad.

Because that's my fourth job: telling stories to Freddy. My father's stories.

A wise, wise person (OK, our dad, the Great Rebus-Maker and Whopper-Teller) once told me that stories are whoppers, but in a good way. My father said there aren't too many stories in the world, and he'd told me practically all of them. But you can tell the same stories over and over by making them different all the time. All you have to do is take pieces of the real world, then string them up in new ways to make a whole other world. My dad told me to do that. He told me to make the stories my own. That's why stories are green whoppers, because they're alive and growing and changing all the time.

The whopper-teller feels good telling the stories. When

my mom makes me wash my Raiders sweatshirt, I lose a little bit more of the smell of my dad. But I still have his stories.

The whopper-getter feels good, too. And eats food of many colors and shapes. And doesn't get real skinny and cry all the time, like he did when the Great Whopper-Teller disappeared forever.

I hand Freddy the plate of fried zucchini. Then I start telling him about our cat Zook's other lives.

* 5 *

Life Number One

MIRACULO AND THE TWENTY-SIX TOES

I pull on my left ear, my story ear, like my father used to do. The ear he pulled when he used to say, "Hey, that reminds me of a story."

Fred leans close to me.

"Once, long, long ago, maybe one hundred years ago or more, there was a fine, fat mother cat," I say. "She lived on a faraway little island called Rebusina. Rebusina was famous for its artists, its olives, and its green vegetables and herbs, especially parsley and zucchini."

My dad's stories took place in Rebusina, so mine do, too. I close my eyes so I can concentrate on the best story-making words, such as *faraway*, *woe*, *befall*, *whence*, and *by and by*.

But I open them a crack to see if Fred is chewing. He is, so I continue.

"One night, when you could see every single star in the sky and the olive groves shimmered in the moonlight, the mother cat gave birth to six kittens under a tree. The smallest one, blue-eyed and black as night, was born last, just as two shooting stars zoomed across the sky. And so it happened that the smallest kitten arrived with two extra toes on each paw, for a grand total of twenty-six. The mother cat didn't care about those extra toes. What's an extra toe or two? Twenty-six toes don't help you dash up an olive tree any better than eighteen, as far as she could tell.

"'I have the same amount of love for all my kittens,' she said. 'OK, maybe I love some a little less than others, but only on the days of the week when they get into scrapes. By the end of the week, it ALWAYS evens out.'"

"Hey, that's what Mom tells us," says Fred.

I open my eyes. "Try to hold your comments and questions till I'm done so I can concentrate, OK? Anyway, lots of mothers say that.

"Every living thing was happy on the island of Rebusina. People burst into song for no reason at all, dancing around the farms as they farmed, like in one of those Broadway musicals. In their spare time, they played musical instruments and painted pictures. They were all kind to one another. Crops grew tall, trees blossomed, insects buzzed, and all the animals did what they were supposed to do—for instance, give milk, run fast, catch mice, whatever. The mother cat's six kittens grew big and strong.

"By and by, something terrible befell the island. There was a drought, a horribly severe one. Rain was badly needed, because everything began withering and drooping in the fields and the groves. The Rebusinians had less to eat and became hungry and grumpy. They stopped having fun. Animals slept more than usual because they were all tired out from looking for food. Butterflies and bees hid.

"The people asked their queen what to do. The queen asked the advice of her Royal Adviser, the villainous Victor. The villainous Victor had a boa constrictor coiled up like a long braid down his back. Whenever advice was needed, the boa constrictor uncoiled itself and hissed smart things into the villainous Victor's ear. Victor, of course, took all the credit. The queen also consulted the young Prince Fredericko and Princess Oonella. But this time, no one knew what to do, even the boa constrictor.

"Then one morning Prince Fredericko woke up and

shouted, 'What a dream I had last night! I dreamt I found a message in a pill bottle, which was floating in the Royal Bathtub. It may tell us how to solve our problem!'

"He wrote down the message on a piece of parchment."

I draw a rebus on my pad.

"OK, try this," I say.

"*L-o-o-k*," reads Fred. "*Look*."

"That's it. Go on."

"*Look 4 . . . Look for! Look for the 26 . . .* What's this supposed to be?"

"A crow."

"*Look for the twenty-six crows?*"

"Right."

I put my rebus-making stuff in my pocket, and Freddy and I start walking out of the alley while I tell the rest of the story.

"So the queen ordered the villainous Victor to crisscross the island looking for twenty-six crows.

"'I deserve a medal for this,' Victor said on his return. 'It was hard tracking down twenty-six, but here they are.'

"Victor released the crows from their cages and they swooped around the Great Main Hall of the castle, and also the smaller, minor halls. Those crows made a HUGE mess. After a week of messes in the castle, nothing had changed in Rebusina.

"'Whence came this dream, anyway?' cried the villainous Victor, swatting at a big crow that was trying to pluck some hairs from his beard for her nest. Victor's boa constrictor whispered into his ear.

"'Off with that dreamer's head!' shouted Victor, looking straight at Prince Fredericko.

"'Ha, ha, don't be silly!' exclaimed the little prince.

"'I know what the problem is,' said Princess Oonella. 'Prince Fredericko forgot to write down the code RW, for "rhymes with *crows*"!'

"So the Royal Family sent out a message to the whole kingdom. Everyone had to rack their brains and think of all sorts of things that rhymed with *crows*—for instance, *bows* and *hoes* and *does* and *piccolos*, which they brought to the castle. It was the villainous Victor's job to organize everything and gather them all together into the Great Main Hall of the castle. Again, nothing changed. The drought continued, with not a drop of rain to be seen anywhere throughout the island.

"'Woe are us!' cried the Rebusinians.

"Then one day, along came a poor zucchini farmer, carrying just one cat.

"'Where are the other twenty-five?' asked the villainous Victor.

"'I've only brought one cat, Your Royal Adviser,' said the farmer.

"Victor's boa constrictor hissed in Victor's ear.

"'*Cat* rhymes with *crows*? NOT!' declared Victor, narrowing his eyes.

"'But—'

"The villainous Victor didn't let the farmer explain further. 'Off with his head!' he shouted.

"'Ha, ha, don't be silly!' exclaimed Prince Fredericko.

"Then Princess Oonella, a good noticer, noticed something incredible.

"'Why, this cat has twenty-six TOES!' she exclaimed. '*Toes* rhymes with *crows*!'

"'You're right!' exclaimed the queen.

"'That's what I was trying to tell you,' said the farmer. 'This is a special cat.'

"'What's so special about him?' asked the villainous Victor. 'OK, he has twenty-six toes. But what does he *do*?'

"All of a sudden: 'EE-OW! EE-OWEY!'"

My dad liked to get a good yell or two in every story to make his audience jump. I like to do that, too. Freddy jumps, but then he laughs.

So I yell again. "'EE-OW! EE-OWEY!'

"That cat had begun to yowl, because he missed his mother and siblings. His yowl was incredibly loud, echoing throughout the Great Main Hall and all the other smaller, minor ones. The yowling was so loud, no one heard the rain-drops at first. But then they heard the earsplitting claps of thunder.

"'HURRAH, HURRAH!' shouted the Rebusinians. 'That cat's yowling caused the rain to fall!'

"Someone found a guitar, and of course there were those twenty-six piccolos, so they had a fantastic party with sing-ing and dancing and pizza in the Great Main Hall, as well as lots of celebrating everywhere else in the kingdom. The rain lasted for a whole week.

"And there's still more to this happy ending.

"The zucchini farmer was given a medal at a special ceremony. The queen announced that the cat was to be called Miraculo and have the honor of residing with them in the castle, as the Royal Cat. Also, the villainous Victor was punished for almost spoiling everything with bad advice. His hours as a Royal Adviser were cut quite a bit. He tried to blame his mistakes on the boa constrictor, but the queen didn't believe him. Anyway, the queen realized she received lots of good advice from her very own children.

"Actually, the ending wasn't *that* happy.

"All day long, Miraculo lounged in the Great Main Hall on a purple velvet cushion, getting fat. Royal Servants brought him tasty tidbits on a gold platter. His favorite tidbit was pizza, which was especially fattening. But soon Miraculo began to miss his former freedom. It was so boring being a rich cat, cooped up inside the castle. Every now and then he'd do his Royal Job, yowling to bring on a rainstorm. But even that got ho-hum after a while. He couldn't run quickly anymore, and he no longer had the energy or the appetite to chase mice on account of his weight gain. Anyway, the Royal Mice-catchers had pretty much gotten rid of all the Royal Rodents. Sadly, Miraculo remembered that chasing mice used to be a whole lot of fun.

"HOWEVER, little did Miraculo realize that he was about to get his freedom in an unexpected way!

"The jealous, villainous Royal Adviser Victor, upon the advice of his boa constrictor, was hatching a villainous plot to kill him.

"In the dead of a Saturday night, when everyone was sleeping soundly after an exciting Royal Ball, Victor tiptoed into the Great Main Hall, where Miraculo lay on his purple velvet cushion. Victor's boa constrictor coiled itself around Miraculo, who was deep in a dream about the finest pizza in the land. Then the snake slithered with the cat into the Royal Aquarium!

"Ahhh. At first the sleepy Miraculo believed he was in the Royal Bathtub. He relaxed his body, making the snake's job very easy. But then Miraculo realized that he was underwater! He couldn't breathe! He twisted and turned and splashed, but he couldn't get free! One, two, three, seven seconds went by, seeming to take forever. The boa constrictor tightened its grip. And Miraculo's fat body went limp.

"Outside the Royal Aquarium, Victor cackled villainously. 'He is now officially the Dead Royal Cat!'

"Not quite! And here is where an extra life or two (not to mention two extra toes on each of your paws) come in very handy: The cat's claws pierced the snake, which loosened its grip. Then Miraculo leaped from the Royal Aquarium, scratching Victor's arms and face.

"'OW! OW!' yowled the villainous Victor, awakening the Royal Guards as well as Prince Fredericko and Princess Oonella.

"'EE-OW! EE-OWEY!' yowled the cat, chasing Victor around and around the Great Main Hall.

"Everyone saw the villainous Victor and his boa constrictor clamber out an open window, followed by the cat.

"But Princess Oonella and Prince Fredericko noticed something INCREDIBLE. That cat was no longer plump and black as night, but teeny-tiny and white as a daytime cloud."

I pause.

I love dramatic pauses. And I am about to say my dad's Three Best Words for story endings. "Always leave the crowd wanting more," he always said.

"Go on," says Freddy.

"To. Be. Continued."

Fred kicks a stone with his sneaker. "Come on! What happens next?"

"I told you," I say. "To be continued."

"But how did they make it rain without Miraculo?"

"Oh, that," I say. "The Rebusinians hadn't needed Miraculo's drought-busting services for quite a while. They'd taught themselves all about proper water conservation in case of another drought."

"Like we did."

"Right," I say.

6

MY NAME THEORY

There is something wonderful and incredible about people's names. You are given a name when you are born, and some people are even given one *before* they are born. Your parents know nothing about you, except that you are very small, know how to yell, need your diaper changed a lot, and enjoy drinking milk. But right away they have to come up with a name for you. I think it may be a law. People have to call you something besides "Hey, you!" all your life.

The wonderful thing is this: After a while, it becomes clear that your name is the perfect name, the only-name-for-you name. Are parents that smart? I don't think so. That's why it's incredible as well as wonderful.

Take my name, Oona. Two O's = two eyes = "noticer." See?

Fred, sometimes Freddy = short, sometimes cute.

My friend Riya loves to sing. Her name is an Indian one that actually does mean "singer." Although it doesn't mean "sings on key," which is a good thing, because Riya doesn't.

Terri, my mom, RW *merry*, which she usually is, except when she's not. But she does try to look merry all the time. The key thing's the look in the eyes—ever notice? I try to keep my mom's eyes looking merry whenever possible.

Max, my dad's name = big, which he was, in heart and spirit and shoe size. No one will ever fill them.

Gramma Dee's name is easy. Dee RW *bee* = honey = sweet like candy. Gramma Dee likes to make Russian taffy, which she learned from her Russian grandmother, who was born in Russia. Although she doesn't make it as often as she used to, because of her concerns about weight gain. And also for dental reasons. That delicious taffy is murder on the teeth, really gluing them together for a few scary seconds. Seven scary seconds almost exactly, if you're counting, which our family always does. I call it the Seven-Second Meltdown Theory. Just when you think your teeth will remain glued together forever, the taffy begins to melt.

On Sunday, I wake up to the wonderful vanilla and butter and sugar smell of Gramma Dee's taffy. Gramma Dee lives down the hall from us, but she makes the taffy at our house. She says that way she can give us a gift: the smell of dad's childhood in our own home. She is famous in our building for her taffy. Maybe even famous on the whole neighborhood block.

I go into the kitchen and there she is checking the taffy with her candy thermometer, a long, clear string of sweet stuff dangling over the pot. Freddy is already there.

"I want a taste!" he says.

"And the magic word is . . . ?" Gramma Dee asks.

"Please!" says Freddy. Gramma Dee swirls a big glob of taffy around a spoon for him to lick. Mom wouldn't approve of taffy for breakfast, magic word or no magic word, but Gramma Dee is different that way. A lot of grammas are.

"We have to save the rest for the celebration today," she says, "at Soma's house."

Soma is my friend Riya's gramma, or *didu*. It's her backyard camellia tree that hangs over the fence, shading our back alley. It was actually Zook who got us all together, back in the days when I wasn't allowed to go around the block by myself yet. Zook was hanging out under Soma's camellia tree, yowling his yowl and pretending to be homeless so Soma would feed him. One day my mom saw Zook eating there and told Soma the truth about Zook. We had a good giggle about that. Now Riya and I are best friends, and so are the two grammas. They spend a lot of time drinking tea, and planning the trips they'll take together when they've saved up enough funds. Soma teaches Gramma Dee words in her Indian dialect, Bengali, mostly food words, such as *aloo* (potato) and *dhoi* (yogurt). Gramma Dee does the same for Soma with her second language, Yiddish. Actually, Yiddish isn't really Gramma Dee's second language, because she only knows a few words from her own grandmother. But she knows all the best words, she says.

"Celebration at Soma's?" I say. "It's hard to think of celebrating at a time like this!"

"I'm glad we have something festive to go to, especially now," says Gramma Dee. "It will take our minds off poor Zook."

"Why do we have to take our minds off poor Zook?" I ask. "I think our minds should be on him every single second, all alone at the vet."

I feel guilty because I really want to go to the party. It will be something special, a Hindu rice-feeding ceremony, called an *annaprasan*, for Riya's baby brother. It will be the first time in his life that he gets to taste solid food.

I go into the hall closet. That's where we keep Zook's litter box. Zook's litter box is the expensive sports car of litter boxes, a real splurge, my mother says. Only the best for our Zook. It has really powerful charcoal odor filters and a cool burgundy trim around its cream-colored body. I pull the chain for the overhead light, close the closet door, and sit on the floor right in front of the litter box. Then I do something really gross. I just can't help myself. I peek inside.

We use special clumping litter for Zook. I see two small clumps near the entrance to the box. Two clumps that poor Zook dragged himself inside to create. I put my cheek against the top of the litter box and think about Zook.

"Where's Oona?" I hear my mother ask.

"In there," Freddy answers.

"In there?" My mother opens the closet door and looks down on me. "Hey, kiddo, get up off the floor," she says softly, and lifts me up. She has just washed her hair and it's all puffed up around her head like a big, curly orange halo. She smells good. My mom wears Beau Soleil perfume, which means "beautiful sun" and must be what Paris, France, smells like on a nice, fine day. Better than Zook's litter box, I have to admit, which stinks. It's my job to clean it, but lately it's hard to throw the clumps away, because they're Zook's.

"I'm not sure I want to go to a party while Zook's in the hospital," I say.

My mother says, "If you don't want to, you don't have to. I'll stay home, too, even though I know we'd both enjoy going. Why don't you think about it a bit? We still have time."

So I go into my room and lie down on the bottom bunk. I look up at the ceiling of my bed, which is the bottom of the top bunk, where Fred sleeps. I'd scribbled the name of My Secret Love there in code. No one in a million years will ever decipher it. Actually, I myself forget which code I used at the time, but that doesn't matter. I know it's him.

I admire My Secret Love because he wears bright shirts with cool patterns that hang to his hips, and he walks as if he's listening to music, which he usually is. I know this isn't what true love is based on. But my parents, the true loves of each of their lives, knew each other for years and years before they knew it was love, so maybe I should just be patient. I'm not sure it's true love that I feel for My Secret Love. Actually, I have no idea what true love feels like. I know that I love my family. I know that I love Zook. But you are not supposed to feel the same way about a boy as you feel about a cat. I believe in true love, just like I believe in magic. Or God. I just haven't had direct experience with true love or magic or God yet.

"Oona?" Fred is knocking softly on the door.

"What?" I say, annoyed, even though it's his room, too.

"I'm wondering what happens next."

"What do you mean?"

"What happens next after Zook—I mean, Miraculo—gets a new life?"

"Not now, Freddy. I want to think about the present-day Zook for a few minutes."

"Oh, OK."

I think about how Zook always knows the exact time we get home at the end of the day, even when clocks are moved backward or forward for the season. There he is at the window, waiting. And I think about how he likes to lap leftover tea from my mother's teacup. And how we snuck him into my dad's hospital room in a basket. That story, especially, keeps playing in my head over and over, like a stuck video.

"Oona?" Fred again.

"What?"

"Are you finished thinking about Zook?"

"Almost."

"Well, are you coming with us to the party?"

"Maybe," I say.

"Hope so," Freddy says.

Freddy really gets inside my heart with those two little words. I know I'm acting like a baby. And all of a sudden, just like that, out of the blue, I get this really good idea: I will donate the secret money we collect from our dancing-in-the-street job to a cat rescue society. I think my good idea is a sign from Zook himself that it's all right to go out and have fun while he recuperates.

I open my bedroom door. My mom is wearing a short lemonade-yellow dress and sandals, but Gramma Dee is wearing the long shimmery blue *sari* that Soma gave her. Some of her stomach is showing. I smile, not because her stomach is funny, but because it's a body part of my gramma I've never seen before.

"OK," I say. "I'm going with you."

And of course I'm wearing my Raiders sweatshirt. My dad always liked celebrating special occasions.

7

MY WISHING THEORY AND MY HOPE-OF-THE-WORLD THEORY

We walk around the block to the party, taking it slow because Gramma Dee isn't used to walking in a *sari*.

Soma's house is dark brown wood with green scallops like half-moons around the windows. There's a twisty buttercup-yellow staircase going up to the pink front door. Riya's mom and dad painted the staircase last month. It took them two whole days, with the help of Riya, her brother Kiran, Mario, and me. I myself suggested the yellow, and Riya picked the pink.

My mother calls it a Victorian. If you stare at the house for a few seconds, then blink quickly a couple of times, it resembles a gingerbread house with frosting. And while you are staring and blinking, what you do is whistle softly or hum under your breath to block out the noise of all the cars going by. You concentrate hard on that scolding squirrel or the squawking hawk high up in the sky. Slowly, slowly you open the iron gate leading to the front walk. The gate creaks nicely. You follow the winding pebbled path to the back of the house and, PRESTO! You are in a magical forest of magnificent old oaks, not someone's backyard near a freeway.

I've taught Freddy to do all this, too.

"Hey, what's up with all the crazy blinking and whistling, you two?" my mother asks.

Gramma Dee pushes away an overhanging vine. "I hope it's not allergies. I told Soma she's getting carried away with this urban farmer business."

"We were just playing a game," I say, and my mother gives me her Look. It's interesting how a Look can say something without words. My mother's Look can mean many things, depending on the situation. This time it says, *Hmmm, should I worry or laugh? I am leaning toward laughter . . . Hmmm.*

Soma's backyard isn't really a forest of magnificent old oaks, because there's only one magnificent oak, a very old one from way, way back when Oakland was a land of oaks.

Oak. Land. Get it? Kiran says it is the oldest oak tree in Oakland. Kiran is always quoting things he's read in books or heard from his parents.

At the other end of the yard, there's that camellia tree, the one shading our alley. Bushy green ferns and shiny leaves of wild ginger grow in the shade, along with a vine winding over the fence. Gramma Dee is right: Soma is an urban farmer. There are tomato plants and rows of lettuces and poles of beans and pepper plants. And there's also Soma's goat, Bleet, and chickens squawking and screeching in a coop, which wouldn't necessarily be found in a magical forest. But then again, as My Secret Love would say, why not?

I wish for a backyard like this someday with all my heart. I've never lived in a house with a backyard, only an apartment with a balcony that has a cactus plant, two chairs, and a barbecue grill on it. Before my dad died, our alley used to be a pretty nice place to call a backyard, until life got in the way. It's still an OK substitute. Still, I've been wishing for a real backyard lately, based on my Wishing Theory:

1. To make a proper wish, you need to designate a Wishing Object, which in my case is Zook's diamond on his old pendant stored in my underwear drawer. Almost anything

can become a Wishing Object if that object is important to you.

2. It is old-fashioned to believe that wishes should be kept secret. Sharing your wish with someone who totally wants the same thing doubles your power. It just makes sense, don't you think? I've shared my backyard wish with my mom, and she says that would be nice, but it's unlikely we'll ever afford one.
3. Impossible wishes do not come true, in my experience. Improbable wishes have a better chance, especially if the wisher has something to do with making them probable. But it's not impossible that our family will have a backyard one day. I'll even take it without a swimming pool.

Seated on blankets in the shade of the oak are zillions of friends and cousins. Some guests are wearing brightly colored Indian clothing, pants and long tunics called *salwar kameez*. Many of the women are wearing *saris* and flowing, beautiful scarves. They look like summer flowers themselves. There's a long, long table covered with bowls of food. And now Gramma Dee's taffy. And pizzas and zucchini from O'Leary's because Maria and Mario are there, too. A few people shout "Go Raiders!" when I walk by and I give them a thumbs-up.

Riya is sitting with Kiran and some of her cousins.

"Hey, Cuzzes," Riya calls to Freddy and me.

Riya calls me Cuz because she says it feels as if I'm her cousin. I like that because I don't have any real cousins. Riya predicts that we actually will be related one day, but she's not sure how. Riya can predict the future by reading the lines on a person's palm, and that's what she says she predicted when she read mine.

Kiran hands me a sheet of blue paper. I notice other guests are holding the same blue papers.

"An information sheet for your edification," he says. "I'm sure you will find it helpful."

On those sheets, Kiran has described the rice-feeding ceremony for those, like us, who have never been to an *annaprasan* before. I'm thinking that maybe we should have had a huge celebration for Freddy, too, the first time he tasted solid food. Maybe then he'd know what a big deal eating should be.

I feel very edified as I read Kiran's information sheet, even though he isn't the greatest speller.

The grandmother makes the infint a special conkoction called payesh, *a mixture of rice, sugar, and water. Then a Seniur Male Member of the mother's family gives the baby his first taste of it.*

Their chubby baby brother, Ravi, doesn't really look as if he's about to eat his first solid meal. He looks very cute in his *dhoti kurta* (*traditionul Indian garb*) and a fancy pointed hat with bangles and balls. He is sitting on his mom's lap beside his dad. They are also wearing beautiful Indian clothing.

Tom, Riya's dad, is of Swedish descent, not Indian descent like his wife, Gitanjali. Riya and Kiran call themselves and baby Ravi "multi-culties."

"We are the hope of the world," Kiran once told me.

That's when I developed my Hope-of-the-World Theory. One day in the distant future, the whole world will be intermarried. Human beings will be like one big happy family and peace will reign among the world's peoples, because everyone will get to understand everyone else's differences, living with them all day long. But then I began wondering how we'd decide which holidays and ceremonies to celebrate since there would be so much good stuff to choose from. We'd be going to parties all the time. Or people could end up fighting about which celebrations to weed out, which would kind of spoil the peace, unless they set up some sort of holiday schedule and took turns. But the more I think about it, the more I realize how much fun it could be.

The Senior Male Member of the mother's family, Riya's uncle Arjun (the one who is in a rock band and plans to move to L.A. to become famous one day), feeds a spoonful of the sweet rice mixture to baby Ravi, who really loves it, opening his little mouth for more. Lots of guests and relatives go up to feed him the *payesh*, and let me tell you, that baby is very happy.

I realize again that I haven't thought about Zook for a while, but this time I don't feel guilty because it's such a beautiful day. All that food smells so yummy, everyone is happy, and the sun is warm on my back. Bleet the goat is nuzzling Freddy's chin and making him laugh.

"Thank you, Zook," I say, because when I got that good idea about giving our job money to the cat rescue society, it was definitely a message from Zook to go out and enjoy the day. Which I am.

Then, just like that, I'M NOT.

Riya is leaping to her feet, running across the yard to

the gate as someone enters the yard from the street. "Uncle Dylan!" she yells.

And Uncle Arjun is at the gate, too, and other guests, laughing and slapping Uncle Dylan on the back, welcoming him back to Oakland after some sort of long trip he took. The sun is in my eyes when I look up, but it's him, all right, with his flashing white teeth and long braid, and a piratey silver earring in his ear. Probably thinks he's the handsomest person in the world.

Dylan.

RW VILLAIN.

Figures!

8

JUST FOR COFFEE

Zook wasn't sending me a message to go to that party. If he was sending me any message at all, which I doubt, it was NOT to go to that party. And to make sure my mom stayed home, too.

Because that's where my mother met the Villain. That's where he kept staring at her and her orangey curly hair, like a big halo around her head. And that's where he smelled her Beau Soleil perfume. And that's where he sang ballads to her with Uncle Arjun's guitar when the sun went down romantically behind the big oak tree and candles were lit in Soma's beautiful garden.

"See? See?" said Riya, watching them. "I told you we

would be cousins. Your mother will become betrothed to Uncle Dylan. I can just tell. The palm never lies."

First of all, Uncle Villain isn't Riya's real uncle, just a singer in her uncle Arjun's band at night. He's a nurse during the day.

Second of all, the whole band will be moving to L.A. soon to try to get famous, according to what Riya has always told me. I reminded her of that.

"Love will always find a way," Riya said.

Baloney. No. Way. My mom and I and Freddy like it here in Oakland, not L.A.

Third of all, palm reading is an inexact science. That's what Gramma Dee says.

Fourth of all, my mother and Dylan are very different people. And I don't mean race or religion, because I happen to really believe in my Hope-of-the-World Theory about the future of the human race. It's just that my mother is a very nice person and Dylan abuses cats. There will be no betrothal between them.

And fifth of all . . . Well, I can't think of a fifth of all, but there must be hundreds of other reasons. My mother will find out herself pretty soon. Tonight, probably. They are out together, but it's not a date.

"We are just going out for coffee," my mother told us. "Gramma Dee's coming over."

"Well, that means you'll be back very early," I said. "We don't need a babysitter."

"Gramma Dee likes being here," said my mother. "She gets lonely."

So here we are, Freddy and I, trying to sleep. Mom's been out a long time. They must be drinking lots of coffee, which is surprising because my mother prefers tea.

This is Zook's third night at the vet. We sure do miss him terribly. I hear the TV in the living room, but Gramma Dee's snoring is the background music. Zook always likes her snoring. He sleeps on her chest when Gramma Dee babysits. But in the deep of night, he comes to sleep with us, starting off on Freddy's pillow, then climbing down to mine at dawn.

I hear Freddy tossing around, kicking off the blankets. I can guess what's coming.

"Oona, what happened next after Miraculo?" he asks. "Please tell me."

9

Life Number Two

JEWEL THE GHOST CAT

OK," I say. "But it's a ghost tale. A scary one. You'd better come down to my bunk for company."

I myself hop out of bed to get a flashlight and my rebus-making stuff from the pocket of my shorts, which I'd flung on a chair. Fred is already in my bunk, all googly-eyed.

"Snuggle up," I say. My dad used to say that before he began a ghost story. I pull on my story ear.

"There was once a very, very old woman and a very, very old man. They lived right smack in the center of Rebusina, in an old dark brown Victorian house with green scallops like half-moons around the windows, and a twisty buttercup-yellow staircase going up to the pink front door. It also had a beautiful backyard garden with a giant swimming pool. The very, very old woman and the very, very old man never had any children. So of course that meant there were no grandchildren, either. But the very, very old woman and the very, very old man didn't mind. They were able to have nice, long, private and pleasant conversations together while drinking mint tea without lots of other people interrupting and shouting over one another, which often happens in big families. They were the loves of each other's lives. The one absolute true love of the other's life forever, until death do them part, and beyond."

"I thought this was a ghost tale," Freddy says.

"I'm getting to that," I say.

"One day, a tiny white kitten leaped into their parlor from an open window. She was as white as vanilla ice cream."

"A *girl* kitten?" asks Fred.

"Shh. Why not?" I ask. "And please stop interrupting." I pull on my story ear again and continue.

"This white kitten, this shy, very quiet kitten had, yes, twenty-six toes. She also had a long, long tail, curled at the tip like a question mark. At the very tip of that tail was a teeny white spot that sparkled like a diamond in the afternoon sun. In fact, it *was* a diamond, or some kind of stone that sure looked like one. The very, very old woman and the very, very old man adopted that kitten and named her Jewel. They grew to love Jewel, even before they discovered the amazing thing about that diamond."

I pause dramatically. "The diamond had the power to fulfill wishes!"

"Wow," says Freddy.

"One day, the very, very old man awoke with a sniffly cold, the kind that gets you sneezing and honking without stop.

"'Mew?' mewed Jewel in her quiet, shy voice.

"'I wish I didn't have this terrible cold!' said the very, very old man, blowing his nose with a tissue. His other hand was petting Jewel, back and forth, back and forth, from her ears to her tail-tip. Then, a few hours later, his cold was gone!

"Another time, the very, very old woman wished she'd remembered to buy butter at the market for her taffy. She was famous in the neighborhood for her taffy. When she got up from petting Jewel, there was a creamy yellow lump on a plate near the sink!

"And one day, the very, very old man wished his favorite striped cap, the only one ever to keep his earlobes warm, wasn't lost anymore. He happened to look up, and there it was, hanging with the soup pot from a kitchen hook!

"Well, the very, very old man and the very, very old woman

soon connected the dots. Every time they touched the diamond on Jewel's tail, Jewel said, 'Mew?' in her quiet, shy voice. And that meant, 'What is your wish?'

"But the very, very old woman and the very, very old man weren't greedy. They already had everything they'd ever wanted—for instance, each other, and also an adorable kitten. And they certainly didn't want Jewel to think they loved her only for the diamond on her tail. So they only wished for improbable things, not impossible ones, which wasn't within Jewel's power to give, anyway. And all their improbable wishes came true."

"What's 'improbable'?" asks Freddy.

"It means maybe it will happen or maybe it won't, and it looks like it won't. But that doesn't mean it's impossible.

"Anyway, one sad day, something terrible befell them. The very, very old woman died, because—well, she was very, very old.

" 'Woe is me!' cried the very, very old man.

"The very, very old man knew that he would die by and by for the same reason, and also because of his broken heart. He and his wife had known each other for ages and ages and were each other's first and only true loves, and one couldn't live without the other.

"So the very, very old man began to make out his will. 'Give all my cash to a cat rescue society,' he wrote. 'Eleven dollars and thirty cents, hidden in my underwear drawer.'"

"Is that where our money is hidden?" Freddy asks.

"Stop interrupting," I say.

"But unfortunately, the very, very old man died right smack in the middle of writing up his will. That's because it took him much longer than necessary on account of all his rebuses."

I switch on the flashlight and reach for my rebus-making materials. I think for a while, write something, then think some more.

"Hurry up," says Fred.

"It's not easy," I say. "I'm having the same problem the old man had, thinking of good ones for you to figure out." I scribble something quickly. "OK, try these. The house goes to . . ."

"*B.* RW hill. *Bill,*" reads Fred.

"Right," I say. "Bill the Butcher. The pots go to . . ."

"*B.* RW hat. *Bat,*" reads Freddy.

"Right. Bat the Baker. And all the furniture goes to . . ."

"*C.* RW fan. *Can. D.*"

"Yup. Candy the Candlestick Maker. And the next part is the most important."

"*We heart our cat. We love our cat,*" reads Fred. "*Do not give her to—*"

"And just at that point, the very, very old man had died. He hadn't had a chance to write 'Dean the mean egg man.' Dean the mean egg man had always snooped around their house whenever he delivered the eggs, asking way too many questions about Jewel's diamond.

"When all the townspeople gathered to read the will, Dean the mean egg man loudly insisted, 'That cat will be happiest in my chicken coop, with hens for company and mice to chase!'

"'Good thinking,' said the mayor.

"Of course, Dean the mean egg man had figured out the wish-fulfilling powers of the diamond.

"Poor Jewel. She spent her days with the mean egg man fulfilling improbable wishes, such as increased egg production whenever she sang to the hens. But one day, the mean egg man locked her up in the silo until she fulfilled some impossible ones: for instance, a golden egg or two. Fulfilling impossible wishes wasn't within Jewel's power to do. And that sad day, inside that silo, brokenhearted, Jewel died trying.

"Just before he buried her in his front yard, the mean egg man snipped the diamond from Jewel's tail. He glued that diamond to a silver pendant attached to a silver chain, which he planned to wear as a bracelet to match the silver earring in his ear. And of course he still planned to enjoy its improbable wish-fulfilling powers, such as increased egg production."

"I thought this was going to be a ghost story," Fred complains again.

"I'm getting to that. Do you think you can take it?"

"Of course," Freddy says. But he snuggles close to me.

"That night, a noise awakened Dean the mean egg man. He sat up in bed.

"'Who's there?' he called.

"There was only the silence of the dark, cold night.

"'Who's there?' he asked again, shivering. And by and by, the answer came.

"'EE-OW! EE-OWEY! I HAVE COME FOR WHAT IS MINE!'

"'What cat is that?' the mean egg man asked. He opened his front door, and seeing no cat, went back to bed. 'I must have been dreaming,' he said.

"But the howling continued. It was 'EE-OW! EE-OWEY! EE-OW! EE-OWEY!' all night long!

"Dean the mean egg man didn't sleep a wink that night.

He even threw a shoe out the window, but that didn't help. The howling went on and on.

"The next night the noise continued, even louder now.

"'EE-OW! EE-OWEY! I HAVE COME FOR WHAT IS MINE!'

"Dean the mean egg man covered his head with his pillow, but he could still hear the howling. There was no sleep for the mean egg man that night, either. He had to take a long nap the next day, and didn't get to feed his chickens or clean out his coops, which decreased egg production quite a bit.

"On the third night, the noise was louder still, almost like the sound of a terrible windstorm.

"'EE-OW! EE-OWEY! I HAVE COME FOR WHAT IS MINE!'

"The mean egg man knew he couldn't afford to lose another night's sleep. He raced to the door and opened it. There was a big, white, see-through Ghost Cat, flashing ghostly teeth and ghostly claws, floating in and out of tree trunks, spinning on the roof, swooping around and around the courtyard, and finally landing on Dean the mean egg man's doorstep.

"'EE-OW! EE-OWEY!' she roared.

"The terrified mean egg man finally remembered the

diamond, which, as you know, was glued to the silver pendant on a bracelet around his wrist. He rubbed that diamond and yelled, 'I wish you'd just shut up!'

"But that was an impossible wish, because no wishes are ever granted if you are rude about it.

"'**SAY THE MAGIC WORD!**' howled the Ghost Cat.

"'What magic word?' asked the mean egg man.

"The Ghost Cat said, '**I SHOULDN'T HAVE TO TELL YOU THAT!**'"

"Everybody knows what it is," Freddy says.

Of course, the Magic Word has been pounded into our heads our whole lives.

"Everybody but Dean the mean egg man," I say.

"The mean egg man tried all sorts of words and groups of words.

"'Abracadabra, shazam, pittooee, frazzlebug, wart of a hedgehog, iddy-biddy kidneys, red monkey guacamole!'

"He tried all night long until he was hoarse, racking his brain to think of all the magic words he'd ever heard in his life. Nothing worked. The loud and annoying howling continued deep into the night.

"'Skedaddle faddle, lizard paddles, hocus pocus, toes on toastus, pokus in the ribus, fee-fi-fo-fum . . .'

"On and on and on, hoarse and exhausted, until finally the Ghost Cat took pity on the mean egg man and gave him a hint.

"'COME ON! THE MAGIC WORD YOUR PARENTS USED TO MAKE YOU SAY!'

"'Thanks?' asked the mean egg man. 'How dee do? Excuse me? Ma'am? Sir? You're welcome? Please pass the pickles? Please? Please! Oh, *that* magic word! OK, I wish you would please, please, please tell me how to make you go away!'

"And Dean the mean egg man's wish was granted. With a sharp claw, the Ghost Cat wrote the answer on a windowpane."

"*The diamond from my . . .*" reads Fred. "*T.* RW pail. *Tail.*"

"Right. Being a Ghost Cat was no life at all, and the Ghost Cat couldn't continue on to her next life without that missing diamond. So the message on the windowpane said, *The diamond from my tail will end this tale.*

"'Here!' shouted Dean the mean egg man, hurling the bracelet with its diamond out the door. 'And I wish I never see you again! Please.'

"The frightened mean egg man (actually, no longer the egg man, since egg production was so small) sold his business and moved far away to live with his sister in Southern Rebusina. He tried to join a rock band. But hardly any rock band needed a tambourine player, which was the only instrument Mean Dean and his Tambourine knew how to play. He did get work every now and then, but mostly then.

"The Ghost Cat was no longer the Ghost Cat or Jewel, but—"

I paused.

"To be continued!" said Freddy.

"Right."

* 10 *

MY CAT-OWNER-VS.-DOG-OWNER THEORY

A father figure is someone who kindly fills in if your father is absent or deceased. For instance, my classmate Carlos has Michael, a Big Brother from the Big Brothers Big Sisters program. Michael takes him to basketball games. He picks up Carlos after school, and they often go pig out on humongous banana splits at Fentons Creamery. I guess Michael's more big brotherly than fatherly, now that I think of it.

My mother has chosen my teacher, Mr. Fry, as my father figure, although she doesn't call him that. She just said she thought it would be helpful for us to have some talks at recess every now and then. I know she wishes he'd tell me to stop wearing my dad's Raiders sweatshirt every day. But we never talk about my sweatshirt. Mr. Fry usually lets me choose the topic.

"Well," says Mr. Fry today.

There are quite a few long, pleasant silences during my talks with Mr. Fry. Mr. Fry is a shy man. (Name Theory: Fry RW *shy.*) Lately we've mostly been talking about cats.

"Zook's still at the vet, hooked up to fluids to flush out his toxins," I say. "His kidneys aren't working well enough to do the job."

Mr. Fry nods. "Well," he says, getting his thoughts together. I study Mr. Fry's cowlick while I'm waiting. It sticks out over his right ear. I figure he tries hard to tame it because it usually looks damp.

"Well. Fluids will certainly help to flush out those toxins," Mr. Fry says finally, nodding his head. "Don't you worry."

I believe him because Mr. Fry himself has three cats.

"My own cat had kidney trouble last year. He was given fluids and he's fit as a fiddle now," Mr. Fry says.

I'm not sure I understand what "fit as a fiddle" means, but I suppose it means that you can get a tune out of it, if it's a fiddle, and that you're back to normal, if you're a cat. Mr.

Fry knows all about tunes, because he plays the cello in the Sailors' Chamber Orchestra. He told us that fact on the first day of school, when he was introducing himself to us.

"I love sailing and movies and mystery novels, and have recently taken up tennis. And I'm allergic to pickles," said Mr. Fry.

"Hoo-hoo, allergic to pickles!" a Rowdy called out from somewhere around Table 2. Our class is made up of Rowdies and Listeners. I'm in the latter group. Rowdies are a few sandwiches short of an all-day picnic, as my dad would have said.

My gramma works in a school office. She knows which teachers keep a lid on things and why. Mr. Fry doesn't know much about keeping lids on. That's why Room 7 keeps boiling over, in Gramma Dee's opinion.

"You don't begin the year trying to be pals with students. You start off firm, set some rules, and then loosen up a bit as the school year goes on," Gramma Dee says.

The Rowdies always talk to one another while he's trying to teach. They throw pencils and rolled-up paper across the room. They mumble "Pass the pickles, please" under their breaths and laugh.

Mr. Fry keeps telling everybody to "keep it down to a dull roar."

My gramma says there shouldn't be any roar at all, dull or any other kind.

"I think it's because Mr. Fry is a cat owner and not a dog owner," I say to Riya and Kiran on the way to pick up Freddy at preschool. Today was a pretty noisy day in Room 7.

"What do you mean?" Riya asks.

Most people would understand exactly what I mean, but Riya doesn't know much about pets. Her parents won't allow them. You have to take off your shoes when you go into their house, and since dogs don't have any shoes to take off, just their big, dirty paws messing up the carpets, that's the end of that.

"Dog owners learn how to be the boss," I explain. "You have to be the alpha with dogs. That means number one. A cat owner doesn't have to learn how to be the boss of its cat. Cats are their own bosses. You can't train a cat to listen to you."

"Just like the kids in the class are the bosses of Mr. Fry," says Kiran. Kiran, a year older than us, had Mr. Fry the year before.

"Right," I say. Even Mr. Fry's cowlick is the boss over him.

Then Kiran says, "You know what? In my opinion, cats aren't as likable as dogs."

What a thing to say, especially to someone whose beloved pet is in the hospital!

"That's not true!" I say, totally shocked. "Of course cats are just as likable as dogs."

Kiran himself wishes his parents would allow them to have a dog. He's read many training books about them in preparation for the future pets he'll have when he's on his own. Every year he watches the Westminster Kennel Club Dog Show on TV. He can reel off the top four smartest breeds (border collie, poodle, German shepherd, and golden retriever) and even tell you what to feed a dog with diarrhea (rice and cottage cheese). He also knows the difference between a domestic and a Persian breed of cat, and a thing or two about scratching posts. But when a person has too much book knowledge and not enough actual experience, their theories can be off base. Way, way off base.

"Cats just don't seem to have that much love or allegiance to their owners," Kiran says.

"Love or allegiance! They have loads of that!" I say. "Right this minute, this very minute, Zook is longing for our entire family."

"Well, you said a cat doesn't obey its owners," says Riya.

"You don't have to command a cat to love you!" I say hotly. "And Zook does love us!"

We have reached Freddy's school. Freddy's face is pressed against the front window, just like Zook's face always is, waiting for us after school. Freddy's school is called the Little Tots Playskool. That's the way they spell it. Playskool. It seems weird that an educational establishment would use the wrong spelling on purpose, but there you go.

We all go into the Playskool, and I put my initials on the sign-out sheet: *O.A*. I make the *A* have a fancy, mature, loopy cat tail, like this:

I am very proud to have the responsibility of signing Freddy out.

And then, walking home, I continue our discussion.

I tell Riya and Kiran how my mom and I smuggled Zook into the hospital to visit my father, the story that's been going around and around in my head these past few days.

"Zook was in a wicker basket covered with a green-

and-white cloth napkin with strawberries on it," I say. "No animals were allowed into the hospital except special therapy dogs, and I don't think there was such a thing as a therapy cat at Kaiser Permanente Medical Center. I had my hand resting on top of the napkin to keep Zook calm so he wouldn't wriggle around. A nurse saw my mom and me and said, 'That looks like a delicious picnic you've got there!' and I said, 'Sure is.' Then we marched right in."

"I thought you said no one saw you go in," Kiran says.

I forgot I'd already told them the story. "Well, I left out that part last time," I say.

I add more details to this story every time I tell it. Every single time I think about it, actually.

"So we went in, and my dad pulled off the napkin and laughed because he was expecting submarine sandwiches or tacos or something. He didn't have much appetite then, anyway. He lifted Zook out. That wasn't easy for my dad to do because he wasn't as strong as he used to be, and Zook is big. But it was worth it, because Zook licked his face all over. Believe me, there was lots of love and allegiance in that bed! He snuggled up next to my dad under his blankets. Zook was purring so loud, like a car motor, or like a refrigerator when you leave the door open, so loud that we had to turn up the radio every time a nurse came into the room. He stayed with my dad for hours and hours."

"Hours and hours and hours," says Freddy, who wasn't even there, but had heard the story a couple of times.

Zook wasn't actually in that bed for hours and hours. Maybe just thirty minutes or so. But it seems like hours and hours every time I think about it. But sometimes it feels like it was just a few minutes. A person's memory is funny that way—ever notice?

"Well, maybe Zook is a special cat," says Riya.

"He sure is," I say.

We say good-bye at Telegraph and 49th, and I'm really not sure if we just had a discussion or some sort of argument. Riya and Kiran and I always have little arguments that blow over without even talking about them again. I guess that's what makes us such good friends.

Fred and I walk by Bank of the West and check it out. No problems there. We don't walk past the Villain's house, because I've seen much too much of him lately. There were two more just-going-out-for-coffees this week.

But, drat, here he is anyway! He zooms over to the curb on his motorcycle and turns into the driveway of our apartment building, right in front of us.

Freddy yells, "DYLAN!"

Major, major caps.

"Would you like to help me wash the bike?" the Villain asks. His silver earring glints in the sunlight.

I shake my head no. Then I narrow my eyes, like that cop on TV. "I've got to go to work at O'Leary's now. So does Freddy."

"Work!" says the Villain, flashing one of his white, toothy smiles. I'm thinking he must spend a fortune on teeth-whiteners. "Do they pay you well?" he asks.

Then Freddy (oh, Freddy!) pipes up. "Yes, they do! We dance and the people on the street give us lots and lots of money."

The Villain gives me a funny look, but I make a face as if I don't understand what Freddy's talking about.

"Let's go, Freddy," I say.

"I don't want to," says Freddy. "I want to help wash the bike."

The Villain lifts Freddy and hugs him. My brother, looking like he's going to faint with happiness, leans against the Villain, and before I can say anything else, they're gliding down the driveway to get the hose from the back alley. Our special alley. The Villain's acting as if he lives with us, using our building's hose. Doesn't he have his own hose at his own house?

I go to work dancing, and even earn a few dollars from some people strolling by.

I've noticed something interesting about dancing: Bobbing up and down shakes up your brain cells, making some of them change places or flip upside down. Well, that's not what really happens, but it sure feels like it. I get excellent ideas for stories while I'm dancing outside O'Leary's, and that's also how I came up with my idea for the Family Straw.

Today, as I dance, I'm thinking I should suggest to Mr. Fry that he ask my mother for tea, not as a husband figure, but as a friend, because she's so lonely. It wouldn't hurt for them to get to know each other. They both enjoy mystery novels and movies, and the right mousse could certainly tame his cowlick, if my mom has a problem with that. Mr. Fry is shy and quiet, not loud and funny like my dad. So maybe Mr. Fry isn't my mother's type. But I never in a million years thought her type was a cat-shooter like the Villain.

I hope Zook is discharged soon, so the truth about the Villain's past (and Zook's) can come out!

* 11

MY SEVEN-SECOND-MELTDOWN THEORY

I return my costume to O'Leary's and go home. My mom is already busy at the stove.

"Freddy's in the back of the building with—" I start to say.

"I know, sweetie," she says. "I got a text from Dylan."

A text from Dylan. How long has the texting been going on? I go into my room and flop down on my bed to do some worrying.

My mom is the fastest, most accurate text-messager in the world. It's this talent she has, she says, with no known benefit to humanity. Here's the thing: My dad and mom knew each other for years and years before they got hitched. But if two people are texting all day long, they could get friendly pretty quickly, even if they're not out together drinking coffee.

The doorbell rings. I hear laughing in the kitchen.

"Dinner, Oona!" calls my mother.

My suspicions are confirmed. She's invited the Villain to dinner. There he is, plopped down comfortably in the fourth chair, where my father used to sit.

"We have a guest tonight," says my mother.

She says that to me in a weird, chirpy voice, as if she meant to say, "We have another guest tonight, just like we always do every single Wednesday night!"

The truth is, we haven't had guests for dinner in a long, long time, except for Gramma Dee, of course, and Riya when she's sleeping over. And never, ever on a school night.

The other strange thing is that my mother has set the kitchen table for a party. Not the kind of party with balloons and party hats, but a fancy dinner party where you use cloth napkins to wipe your mouth. In this case, lacy green-and-white napkins with strawberries hand-stitched around the borders, the ones that used to belong to my mother's great-aunt Rose. They are kept with old tablecloths and coasters in a special drawer in the kitchen, a drawer that always smells perfumey, like long-ago celebrations. But we never use the napkins at dinner because they're not permanent press, my mother always says, and who has time to iron in this day and age?

"I'm glad to be here," says the Villain. "I usually eat alone."

I am speechless, although I'm the only one who is. Freddy is yakking away about that motorcycle. The Villain is yakking about it, too: how it took him and his guitar all the way cross-country and back, and how he stopped to sing in bars and cafés and work as a nurse in hospitals along the way. My mother is asking him questions about that trip like he'd been to the moon or something.

"It's good to be back in Oakland," says the Villain. "And it's nice to have a home-cooked meal with all of you. I can't believe we've never met. I've lived on Clover Street almost all of my life."

He takes his napkin and spreads it on his lap. Under normal circumstances, I'd have a good, loud laugh right about now at the expense of this piratey person in old jeans and cowboy boots, a lacy napkin on his lap.

I don't feel like laughing. The truth is, I feel like throwing up. Especially when my mother brings dinner to the table.

"Please don't hold this against me," says my mother in that new, chirpy voice of hers. "I didn't have the time to cook, so

I picked up something from Farmer Joe's take-out counter called Mediterranean Chicken with Chick, Peas, and Urb Sauce. Doesn't that sound good?"

"More than sounds good. Man, it looks and smells wonderful," says the Villain.

"Wonnerful!" says Freddy, chirping like my mother.

CHIRPING is an important word here.

My mother has gone too far. Not only is she pretending she has lots of time to iron fancy napkins, but now she's pretending she has lots of money to spend on gourmet food that she didn't even make herself! "If you make it yourself, it's half the price," she's always told us.

And what does she buy at that gourmet counter? Something disgusting! Except for Gramma Dee who doesn't eat meat (although she does eat smoked fish once in a while), we're all meat eaters around here, and I do sometimes feel guilty about that. Meat eaters don't usually think about what they are eating, but you can't help it when your dish has a title. Chicken with Chick! I squeeze my eyes shut.

"Oona, why are you making faces?" my mother asks.

"I'm not eating that," I say.

"And why not, may I ask?"

"Do you really expect us to eat a mother hen lying in a

sauce with its baby?" I ask. My eyes are still closed. I can't bear to look.

"What are you talking about?"

There is a pause, and I hear choking sounds coming from my mother. My eyes fly open, and there she is, not choking, but trying her hardest not to laugh. The Villain has his head down, examining a strawberry stitched on his napkin.

"Honey," says my mother. "Not chicken with *chick*! Chicken with *chickpeas*. Garbanzo beans. You've had them before. And Riya's *didu* puts chickpeas in so many of the Indian dishes you like."

"I love garbanzos," says Freddy, popping one into his mouth with his fingers. Then he starts wolfing down that chicken like he's in some sort of chicken-eating contest or something. And there are flecks of GREEN on top of the chicken, which he doesn't even seem to notice.

"Oh, of course. Garbanzos," I say. "Well, I've never eaten urb sauce before."

"Oona, you know you have!" my mother says. "Since when are you such a picky eater?"

The Villain starts talking about the garden he's digging in his backyard and all the tomatoes and urbs he's planting, rosemary and parsley and oregano, and I suddenly realize that they mean "herbs"! Except they're using a show-offy accent: dropping the "h" and calling them "erbs."

"You mean 'herbs,'" I say, wriggling my pointer fingers as I say the word.

"Erbs," says my mother, wriggling her own fingers. "You're not supposed to pronounce the 'h.'"

Well, how was I supposed to know that? I'm sure many people go around for years and years thinking the wrong things about words like *herbs*, words they've only read in books and never said out loud until they have a dinner dish with a title. Take the word *humiliated*, for example. It starts out "hyoo," not "hum," like I used to think it was. That's exactly how I feel. HYOO-miliated, especially because he's here. And there's my mother, smiling at the Villain over my head.

"Fresh herbs are easy to grow," the Villain says. "You could put some in those blue pots you have in the alley out back. Lots of sun there. You'd have yourself a nice kitchen garden. It could look really nice. You kids and I could do it as a project together."

"That's a great idea! Isn't it, Oona?" my mother chirps, as if it had never, ever looked beautiful back there until life got in the way! As if no one had ever suggested planting something in those pots again. For example, me.

"We'd need to do a lot of watering for that," I say. "We're trying to conserve."

"Rosemary doesn't need much water," the Villain says.

"Anyway, I don't have the time for extra projects," I say.

"I have the time!" says Freddy.

I glower at my brother. My mother starts to say something, but the Villain holds up his hand and she doesn't. "That's OK, Oona," he says. "Maybe another time."

My mother brings out dessert, store-bought chocolate graham crackers and Gramma Dee's taffy. We all pop a piece of taffy into our mouths. We chew and chew. The taffy glues my teeth together. I count to seven in my head.

"Hooray!" my mom and Freddy and I shout at the exact same time, when that taffy finally melts. Just like we always do.

The Villain, still chewing, looks perplexed. "Am I missing something?" he asks.

My mom explains the Seven-Second Meltdown Theory, and he tells her his own taffy hasn't melted yet.

"It only works for family members," I say coldly.

"I see," mumbles the Villain, his teeth still stuck together.

"Oh, Oona," says my mother.

I suddenly feel ashamed. I look down and a couple of tears

plop onto my plate, salting those chocolate graham crackers. Nobody sees. The reason I feel ashamed is because I notice something different about my mother, something I noticed as soon as I walked into our apartment today but didn't want to admit. It's this: My mother looks happy. Happiness is all over her. Her fingers are happy, holding the fork to her happy mouth. Her elbows on the table are happy. Her shiny orange hair is shooting off happiness sparks, pulled up in a new happy hairstyle. And her eyes; her eyes are happy. I'm sad because I realize her eyes haven't looked like that for a long time. And it's the Villain who's making her feel that way.

All of a sudden my imagination revs up something awful. I start imagining that he and my mother actually do get married. There we all are at the same table, slurping liquid through a gigantic Family Straw. The only one not using the straw is the baby banging a spoon in its high chair, because, of course, if the Villain and my mom got married, they'd have one of those. An adorable baby with skin the color of taffy, a multi-culty baby, a hope-of-the-world baby, whom my mother may love a bit more than Freddy and me for that exact reason.

* 12

MY DESPERADO THEORY

Sometimes a revved-up imagination is useful. I did come up with one great idea last night, even though I realize that it's a crime:

I will cat-nap Zook from the vet.

I didn't really have a plan at first. In fact, I wasn't even thinking about smuggling *out*. I was thinking about that time Zook was smuggled *in*. In to the hospital to visit my dad, Zook all covered up by a green-and-white napkin with tiny red strawberries stitched around the edges, one of the special-occasion napkins that belonged to my mother's great-aunt Rose.

"This picnic for your father is a special occasion," my mother had said.

My father had lifted up one corner of that napkin, and when he saw Zook inside, he said, "What's this? A furry taco?" We cracked up at my father's joke, my mom and I, giggling like goofballs.

Of course, his joke wasn't *that* funny. My dad was capable of much more hilarious jokes, believe you me. It's just that he hadn't made a joke for a while, and it really felt like old times, good times, again. I guess that's why I keep thinking about that morning in the hospital over and over.

Anyway, today I'm dancing at O'Leary's while planning and remembering all of this. The song playing on Mario's boom box is "I Heard It Through the Grapevine," sung by Marvin Gaye. I like that song, and all of a sudden, it has personal meaning for me, like some sort of sign that my cat-napping plan is a good one. My mother says that the best songs have personal meaning for you. In this song, a guy is complaining because someone tells him that his love prefers someone else, someone she used to love before.

Don'tcha know that I heard it through the grapevine,
Not much longer would you be mine!

I start imagining the Villain singing those words. The Villain sounds like Marvin Gaye when he sings, in my mother's opinion. But it won't be the grapevine telling my mom the truth about the Villain. And it won't be me taking away her happiness. It will be Zook himself. Actually, the Villain himself, confessing all when confronted with Zook in my arms.

THE VILLAIN (reeling backward in total shock): Why—why—it's my old cat, Mud!

ME: Yes, it's him all right, you cat-shooter, you!

THE VILLAIN (beginning to tremble and sweat): How—how do you know all that?

ME: I have my ways! I know everything!

MY MOM (forehead wrinkled with confusion): I don't understand! How could he be your old cat? Why are you trembling and sweating? Oona, what do you mean by "cat-shooter"? And our cat's name is Zook!

ME (looking at the Villain and narrowing my eyes): Go ahead. 'Fess up!

I'm not sure if the Villain will confess everything or not. Time will tell. But his behavior will alert my mother to his real character. She'll know something is fishy. They'll part ways, and then I'll tell her all the terrible details. She'll probably thank me.

And now that I think of it, cat-napping Zook won't be a crime because the stolen goods belong to me in the first place. I have a plan, too. I'll remove the screen I just happened to notice in the window over Zook's cage. Then I'll tell a big blue whopper. I'll say that when Zook smelled his beloved owner walking by, he jumped up, clawed through the screen, and leaped out the window. Just like Miraculo/Jewel did in my story for Fred! My dad always said that art imitates life. This will be life imitating art. Well, actually, a blue whopper imitating my story, a green whopper.

Except now I just realized I'll have to come up with another plan. There's probably an alarm on that window.

I begin to wonder if all crimes start this way. For instance, bank robberies. Maybe the bank robbers aren't bad guys to begin with, just people who can't get good jobs. They start imagining an easy way to get money to buy food for their families or gifts for their younger brothers and sisters, and before you know it, they've worked out a plan. In their minds, the plan is foolproof and no one will get hurt, and as soon as things get better in their lives, maybe they'd even give some of the money back.

I mention my theory about bank robbers to Mario while Freddy and I are having our Daily Slice at O'Leary's. Fred's also wolfing down a big plate of zook.

Mario pinches his nose a few times with one hand, a sign that he's thinking about the topic at hand. Mario is another one of my father figures, but I chose him myself. Mario is very wise. Not only as a pizza businessman, but in lots of other ways. He never had a chance to go to college, but he is an *autodidact*, he told me. An autodidact is a person who has taught himself most of what he knows, and Mario knows a lot, believe you me. I would like to be an autodidact, too—shorten my hours at school, learn whatever I like, whenever and from whomever I like. Kind of like a school furlough. Of course, my mother disapproves.

"People do things they wouldn't ordinarily do when they're desperate," Mario says about those imaginary bank robbers. "That's why we call them *desperadoes*. They are doing something rebellious for a very good, understandable reason."

That's so Mario! Wise and kind at the same time.

Desperado is a good word.

Meanwhile, Freddy keeps jumping up to look out the front door of the store every time he thinks he hears a motorcycle pulling up.

"Freddy, sit down and eat!" I say.

Mario gives me a quick, sharp look, and I know he's wondering why I'm snapping at my brother. I never, ever snap at Freddy that way, but I can't help it today.

"Freddy is obsessed with motorcycles lately," I say. "It's a bit unhealthy, in my opinion."

"Maybe it's Dylan he likes?" Mario asks.

"No, it's the motorcycle," I say.

But I know Mario is right, as usual.

I have so many questions about love! What makes it true, and what makes it not-so-true? Why does love seem so hard, and why is almost every single song about love so sad? I don't want to make my mother unhappy. But shouldn't she find out the truth?

And what about Freddy's little hurting heart?

I want to ask Mario's advice, but there just isn't time. Hundreds and hundreds of lovey-dovey texts are probably zooming back and forth between my mother and the Villain right this very second.

I jump up from my seat. "We have to go home now," I blue-whopper. "My mother is coming home early."

"That's nice," says Mario.

I saw the Villain put his hand on my mom's shoulder when they were washing dishes together last night. Things are happening way, way too quickly. I am a DESPERADO!

"Come, Freddy," I say. I grab his hand, and out the door we go.

13

MATILDA AND ZOOK

"Where are we going? Why are we rushing?" Freddy asks. His short legs are pumping away because I'm walking so fast, almost running.

"We're not rushing," I say.

"Yes, we are," he says, panting a bit.

He's right. It feels like a big whoosh of wind is blowing me down the street. I want to get started on my new plan before I lose my nerve.

"OK, we're going to the vet and I'm rushing because I want to get there before visiting hours are over," I say.

"I didn't know there were visiting hours at the vet," says Fred.

Actually, no one had mentioned anything about visiting

hours. I'd even looked for a big sign announcing the hours, like the sign on the wall at the hospital where my father had been, but I hadn't seen one at the Good Samaritan Veterinary Clinic.

"Of course there are visiting hours!" I say, and the thought that there really aren't makes me angry. I walk even faster.

We've reached the clinic. We go up the front stairs, then through the big glass doors.

There are two Good Samaritan receptionists at the front desk. I notice that one of them is wearing a T-shirt that says DOG IS GOD SPELLED BACKWARD. Under normal circumstances, I'd want to spend some time pondering that, but now all I have time to think about is Zook and my plan.

PLAN

STEP ONE: Freddy and I somehow stroll through the door toward the examining rooms.

STEP TWO AND ALIBI: If someone questions us, we and our mom brought our gerbil in for a regular exam. We're just strolling the hallway while we wait for it to be examined, that's all.

STEP THREE: Hunt for the big room where all the overnighters are kept.

STEP FOUR: Find it.

STEP FIVE: Somehow free Zook and somehow hide him under my sweatshirt and smuggle him out, just for a few hours or so.

PROBLEMS: Too many "somehows."

"May I help you?" asks a receptionist, not the one wearing the DOG IS GOD SPELLED BACKWARD T-shirt. This one is wearing dangly, sparkly earrings with circles and spokes. They look like cat toys, and under normal circumstances I'd probably warn her about those earrings. Not the greatest fashion choice if you work around cats.

Instead, I say, "We're waiting to meet my mother. She's parking the car. She'll be here in a few minutes with our sick gerbil."

Freddy turns toward me, his eyes popping out of his head. Even Freddy, who believes almost everything, gets that this is a great big whopper.

"Do you have an appointment?" Sparkly Earrings asks.

"It's an emergency," I say. "He was turning as purple as an eggplant and throwing up and seeing double. So we came right over."

"Oh, my," says Sparkly Earrings.

"His name is Matilda," I continue, sitting down on the scratched red couch. "We thought he was a girl at first, that's why he's called Matilda. It's not easy figuring out those kinds of things with gerbils. Of course, we couldn't tell for sure that he was seeing double, except that he kept nibbling on an invisible garbanzo bean and an invisible carrot stick near the real garbanzo bean and carrot stick. He also smells funny."

I figure if I give lots of details, my story will sound real and true. I learned that from my father.

I continue. "Matilda smells like pot roast. It's weird."

"And also pickle pancakes," says Freddy, really getting into the blue-whopper thing. I know my brother very well. The poopy jokes will be next.

Sparkly Earrings doesn't help matters. "Maybe Matilda ate something that's upset his little tummy," she says.

"Maybe," I say, frowning at Freddy.

"He's really poopy!" Freddy says, giggling. "Super-duper stinky poopy!"

I ignore him and try to look worried about Matilda for the both of us, easy to do because I'm worried about a real patient named Zook. And worried about my plan, too, which seems silly now, in real life. Not to mention almost impossible. The last time I'd been at the Good Samaritan Veterinary Clinic, it had been very busy. I'd felt practically invisible. It's not busy at all today, and Freddy and I aren't invisible.

"SUPER-DUPER STINKY POOPY!" shouts Freddy. He has his head in my lap. He's giggling so hard, his nose is running.

"Shh," I say. "This is a hospital." I try to smile maturely at Sparkly Earrings. "He's only five."

"I understand," she says kindly. "I have one of those five-year-olds at home." She looks at my sweatshirt. "Go Raiders!"

Freddy sits up. "Is it visiting hours yet?" he asks her.

"There are no visiting hours, dear," Sparkly Earrings says.

"Oona says there are."

"There are no specific hours," Sparkly Earrings says, and then to my great surprise, she adds, "but if Matilda is admitted you can visit him whenever you like. Within reason, of course."

Turns out we could have visited Zook himself anytime we wanted to. I didn't need to invent a Matilda after all. Too bad. I was sort of getting to like him.

"We want to see Zook!" says Freddy, jumping up. "Right now!"

I explain who Zook is and that he's one of their patients,

getting all his toxins flushed out because of his kidney problems.

Dog/God narrows her eyes suspiciously, just like a cop. "My, my. Your family isn't having much luck with its pets lately," she says.

I nod. "It's been a bad week."

"Mom must be having trouble finding a parking place," Dog/God continues.

"It's so hard to find parking in this city!" says Sparkly Earrings.

Dog/God is suspicious, but I think Sparkly Earrings believes my whoppers. It's hard to tell. I remember that there are usually two cops at interrogations, one nice and one not-so-nice.

But then Sparkly Earrings says, "I'm sure it's OK to visit Zook while you're waiting for your mother and Matilda."

She gets up to open a door in the far corner of the waiting room and waves a hand for me and Freddy to follow her. We go down a bright hallway with doors on either side. Those doors lead to the examination rooms I'd been in a few times at Zook's regular visits. Photos of healthy-looking dogs, cats, and birds line the pink walls. They're all so happy, they actually look as if they're grinning into the camera. There are also photos of ratlike creatures that are gerbils, hamsters, or guinea pigs, I'm not sure which. If I really owned a Matilda I could probably tell the difference. I start worrying that Sparkly Earrings will ask me some test questions about the differences between gerbils, hamsters, and guinea pigs, but she doesn't.

I don't know where those happy photographs came from, because next thing you know, we're in a large room filled with the gloomiest animals I've ever seen, mostly dogs and cats, each lying in its own lonely cage. There's a parrot in one cage with a bandage over its eye, looking perky and piratey, except that it's huddled in a corner, still as a statue. The air smells like a mixture of alcohol and something like bananas, a sweet smell which seems to be trying to hide all that sadness. A tall, skinny guy with spiked purple hair is counting pills at a counter.

Suddenly, I hear Zook. I'd know his Zook yowl anywhere! He knows we're here! I whirl around.

"Zook!" Freddy and I cry out at the same time.

We rush to his cage. Sparkly Earrings opens the cage door, reaches in for Zook, and hands him to me. "I'm going back to the front desk now. This is Boo. He'll help you if necessary."

Boo with the spiked hair grins at us, a friendly gap between his two front teeth. "That old guy's sure glad to see you! Let me know when you're done hugging him and I'll put him back."

We will never, ever be done hugging Zook. I bury my nose in his fur, smelling that alcohol-banana smell. Freddy strokes his nose. Right now there's no other sound in the room except for Zook's purr. It's like a song I love that I haven't heard in a while, even more beautiful than ever.

Boo is murmuring something to a little brown poodle in its cage. The dog's stumpy tail wags feebly. Now that I'm holding Zook, the other animals don't seem so sad anymore. Just tired and sick. There is a difference.

Actually, Zook looks much better. His eyes stare right into mine, bright and clear. His tail is high and happy. It feels like he's gained some weight around his middle.

Now Boo is leaning way down, giving that poodle an injection.

I've done this smuggling stuff before. I can do it again. Smuggle in, smuggle out; same thing. It'll only be for an hour or so, and then we'll bring him back.

Quickly, I stretch out the front of my Raiders sweatshirt

and cover Zook. I can almost hear my dad saying, "Atta girl! Go for that touchdown!" I knew there was an important reason for wearing his sweatshirt!

I put my finger to my lips. "Shh!" I whisper to Fred, who's got that bug-eyed look again.

Slowly, slowly, Fred and I do some sidling along the wall. Boo isn't paying attention to us. He has a lot going on. I have my hands over my sweatshirt. The door is partly open. I open it all the way with my shoulder and we step out into the hallway. How easy was that?

Except that Dog/God is waiting for us.

14

MORE SECRETS

"EE-OW! EE-OWEY! EE-OW! EE-OWEY!"

I will never, ever forget Zook's wail, that long, long, sad and disappointed wail he made when Dog/God took him away from me and Boo put him back into his cage.

Mom came to pick us up at the vet. After she'd made us both apologize to the two receptionists, all she said was, "Let's go."

Then . . .

SILENCE.

Here we are, me and Freddy, in the backseat of the car. We're holding hands. We're in big trouble. OK, it's mostly me who's in trouble, when you come right down to it. I am looking at the back of Mom's head as she drives. Even the back of her head looks angry. Her orange curls seem coiled tighter than ever. The Villain's beside her, fiddling with the radio.

But I don't hear the music, or the traffic, or the air that always whistles through the back window on my side, the window that's stuck because Mom can't afford to fix it right now. All I can hear is Zook's wail, even though we're heading home and he's back at the vet's for more kidney flushing.

I take that back. I can hear Mom's silence. Silence has a sound—ever notice? Mom's silence sounds like a drum. THUMPA-THUMPA-THUMPITY-THUMPA. You can really hear it if you're in big trouble in the backseat of her car.

We slink into our building behind Mom and the Villain. Thumpa-thumpa-thumpity-thumpa, even in the elevator going up. And also the sound of Zook's sad EE-OWEY in my head.

The Villain clears his throat. "Need a new lightbulb in here," he says, looking up at the elevator ceiling.

He's right, but now isn't the time for a lightbulb discussion. My mother frowns and looks straight ahead. The Villain puts his hand on Freddy's head and Freddy smiles up at him.

"We saw Zook," Freddy says. He's already forgotten he's in trouble.

"I know you did," says the Villain, and lifts Freddy up. My mom and I don't say anything.

Inside, Mom herds me to the living room couch. The Villain and Freddy go into the kitchen. It's clear I'm the only one who has a problem here. I hear the Villain opening the fridge. Our fridge.

My mother sits in an armchair across the room, staring at me. Thumpa-thumpa-thumpity-thumpa. Finally, finally she speaks, but in a sad voice, not an angry one. All of a sudden I realize I like it better when my mom is angry.

"Oona, Oona," she says. "What were you thinking?"

Well, that, ladies and gentlemen, is a big question. I was thinking lots of things! Dumb things, I guess. But right now I'm thinking about only three. Number one: Zook's wail. Number two: Zook's old collar. *Mud's* collar, that is. Number three: It's time. Time to tell my mom everything, no matter how happy she is with the Villain. She has to get over him! And she will when she learns the truth.

My mother leans toward me. "Do you realize how bad Mario feels?" she asks. "We spoke to him from the car on the way to pick you up. He trusted you, Oona. You told him you were going straight home."

Mario.

"Oh," I say.

"And that nice Evelyn, too."

"Who's Evelyn?"

"The receptionist at the vet. She trusted you, too. I hope she doesn't get into trouble for this."

"Oh," I say. "Like lose her job?" If she's the trusting one, it was Sparkly Earrings.

My mother shrugs. I hear a kettle shrieking in the kitchen.

I'm thinking that Dog/God probably snitched on Sparkly Earrings. Probably told Mom about Matilda, too. And all of a sudden, I understand that T-shirt, DOG IS GOD SPELLED BACKWARD. If God is so wonderful, like most people think God is, and if dog is God spelled backward, then dogs are pretty wonderful, too. So I'm wondering if Dog/God thinks dogs and other animals are more wonderful than people. That's why it's not a big deal for her to snitch on a friend. Or not trust two kids who miss their cat.

Of course, she had a reason not to trust us. But still.

"And then, miss, there's that little matter about the money," says my mom, looking more deep-down sorrowful than ever.

"The money?" I'm stalling. "What money?" There could be a teeny chance she doesn't mean *that* money.

She does. "The money you got dancing outside O'Leary's."

I hear the Villain talking on the telephone as if he lives here. I feel something like a hot balloon filling up my chest.

"Who told you?" I ask. "It was the Villain, right?"

Oh, I didn't mean to call him that! The hot balloon had suddenly burst inside of me, and out popped that name. But now that it's out, I can tell my mother everything.

She falls back against the armchair as if I'd thrown something across the room at her. "What did you say?" she asks. "*What* did you say?"

But she knows. She stares at me, understanding. "His name is Dylan, Oona. Dylan. And no, it was Freddy who told me, on the way to school this morning. The money you've hidden in your underwear drawer."

I jump up and go over to her chair. Now is the time. The only question is whether to tell her about the Mud collar in private, or confront the Villain with it, too. I decide to do it now, privately. We can have a good cry about the whole thing together.

"I have to tell you something important," I say. "Very important."

My mother doesn't seem to hear what I'm saying. "I suppose it's my fault," she says. She has this faraway look in her eyes, and she's staring at the wall like she's watching a tear-jerking movie that only she can see. "I've been too lax." She leans over and gently tugs the bottom of my Raiders sweat-shirt. "It's time to talk about your fashion choices, too," she says with a big sigh.

"No! We've already talked about that. I like my fashion choices," I say, stepping back. No fair bringing my dad and his sweatshirt into any of this, as if any of it's his fault!

That's when Freddy and the Villain come into the room. The Villain puts a cup of tea on the little table beside Mom's chair. I can smell it. Mint. There's a slice of lemon on the saucer, sweet and sour, just the way my mom likes her tea. I don't know how he knows that, if they're out drinking cof-fee all the time. And there's Freddy drinking a can of apricot nectar through a straw, our favorite drink, which we are only allowed to have every now and then because of the empty calories and the fake apricot from chemicals. The Villain hands me a can with a straw in it, too. I almost refuse, but I'm so thirsty. I take a few fast slurps. It goes down easy. Empty calories taste so good when you're down in the dumps—ever notice?

Now the Villain is whispering something in my mother's

ear, lovey-dovey-like. My mother says, "Oh, I don't know if that's the right thing to do."

"Do what?" I ask. I hate secrets, except, of course, if I'm the one keeping them. I know that sounds babyish, but that's the way I feel right now.

The Villain says, "Terri, I think it will be a good thing."

"Let's talk about it in the car. I'll ask Dee to sit," she says. Her mouth is a firm, straight line as she phones my gramma to come over.

"Talk about what?" I ask when she gets off the phone.

My mother looks at me for a few seconds. She opens her mouth to say something, then changes her mind. The buzzer rings. Gramma Dee. Mom takes a few gulps of mint tea and wipes her mouth with the back of her hand. "Nothing," she says. "We'll be back in a little while."

I can't help myself. I stare straight at the Villain with cop eyes, and out of my mouth come a bunch of big caps. "HIS REAL NAME'S MUD!" I yell.

The Villain's own eyes look hurt, not like the eyes of a guilty person ready to confess. Of course, he's probably a trained actor. Singer-guitar players often are.

My mom, though, looks angry again.

"I mean—" I say. "Zook—"

My mother grabs me and pulls me toward her. Even if I tried to say more, it would come out all muffled. "Oh, Oona. Enough," she says, and then they're out the door.

15

Life Number Three

BEAU THE FLYING CAT

I'm too angry to fall asleep, so I decide to tell Freddy the Splat story. I'm angry at Freddy, too, for spilling the beans about the money. But I don't want to come right out and say that. I don't like being angry with my brother. So I decide to tell him the Splat story, which is perfect for the situation.

I climb up the ladder and shake him gently. "Wake up, Fred. Time for another story. The Splat story. I'm turning on the light so you can see the rebuses."

Freddy sits up, all googly-eyed, ready to listen. Five-year-olds are either awake or asleep—ever notice? Nothing in the middle.

When my father told me the Splat story for the very first time, I was very little, maybe four or five, like Freddy. His story was about a vain tortoise who couldn't keep a secret. Mine will be about a vain cat who couldn't keep one.

"Once there was a cat named Beau Soleil, who used to be named Jewel," I begin. I pull on my story ear. Fred leans against me.

"Beau Soleil, or Beau for short, was beautiful, maybe the most beautiful in Eastern Rebusina. He had a big, wide forehead that made him look wise, and eyes like two shiny suns. His coat was a soft gray, like a rain cloud. The diamond on the pendant around his neck looked even shinier against his fur. His legs were skinny, but long and muscular.

"Beau knew how handsome he was. As he traveled across Eastern Rebusina on his long, strong legs, birds twittered, and bees buzzed. Cows mooed, and donkeys lifted up their heads to bray. Like this: 'HOO-HAH!'"

Freddy giggles. "Did Beau have twenty-six toes, too?" he asks.

"Of course," I say.

"'Who is that handsome cat?' the creatures all said.

"'It's me, Beau. Why, thank you!' Beau would purr

modestly, as if being beautiful were a big surprise to him. He didn't want them to think he was conceited.

"Beau liked to look deep into his own yellow eyes whenever he stopped for a drink at a pond.

"'Ahhh,' he said. 'Who is that handsome cat?' Then Beau would yowl, because he wasn't surprised at all, 'It's me! It's me! It's me! EE-OW! EE-OWEY!'

"One day, while admiring himself in a pond, Beau met one big goose and one medium-size one, shading themselves in a pickapoo grove at the pond's edge.

"'Hello,' said the bigger of the geese. 'How handsome you are!'

"'Why, thank you!' purred Beau, pretending to be surprised.

"'And you look very wise, too,' said the other goose. 'Wise enough to keep a secret.'

"'Secrets are fun to share,' said the bigger goose. 'As long as they are kept.'

"'Oh, I love secrets!' said Beau.

"'But can you keep one?' asked the medium-size goose.

"'Of course I can keep a secret!' yowled Beau, although he wasn't really sure.

"'*Shh!*' honked the bigger goose. 'Secrets travel quickly through the pickapoo vines! OK, here is the secret: We are about to go to Western Rebusina!'

"'What's so wonderful about Western Rebusina?' asked Beau.

"'*Shh!*' honked the medium-size goose. She looked around to see if any others were listening. 'Western Rebusina is bigger and better than Eastern Rebusina. There are huge lakes rather than little ponds. There's lots of rain, the grass is always green, and yellow yarrow and strawberries cover the fields. Purple catmint flowers, too!'

"'Yum,' purred Beau, who had a wonderful appetite.

"'Best of all,' said the bigger goose, 'Western Rebusina is practically empty! All that good stuff, just for us. And it will stay that way, as long as you don't blab away our secret.'

"'I've already told you, I can keep a secret!' said Beau. 'Where is this wonderful place?'

"'We have a map from a red-billed yaba-blabba bird, who shared the secret with us. But really, this is as far as it goes. We can't have anyone else finding out about it.'

"The geese showed Beau the map. It was written in code."

I write down the directions for Freddy.

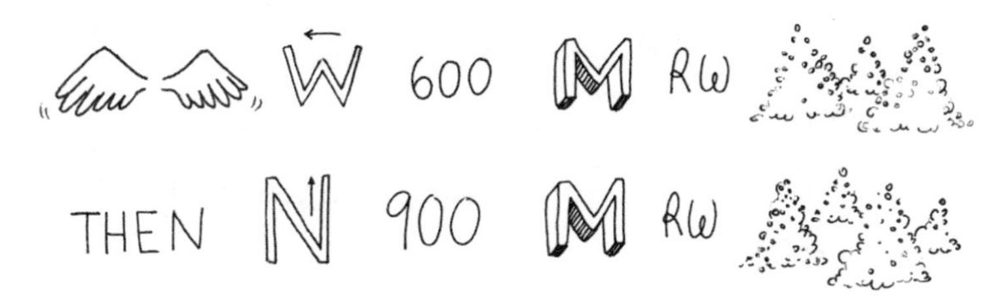

"*Wings*," says Freddy. "Then the letter *W*."

"Come on, what do wings help you do?"

"Fly!"

"And *W* means *west*."

"*Fly west six hundred.* Six hundred *M*. What's that?"

"Piles. Six hundred, and now think of something that starts with *M* and rhymes with 'piles.'"

"Oh. Miles. *Fly west six hundred miles. Then N, north, nine hundred miles!*"

"'Six hundred and then nine hundred!' yowled Beau. 'It will take me forever to get there!'

"'Not if you fly!' said the medium-size goose.

"'But I can't fly,' said Beau.

"The geese looked astonished. 'You can't fly? Why not?'

"'I guess because I don't have any feathers,' said Beau.

"'Oh, that's easily fixed,' said the bigger goose. 'I have lots of extras.'

"'Me, too!' said the medium-size goose. 'We'll just stick them on you with pond mud and pickapoo sap. And we'll stick the map of Western Rebusina onto your belly in case we get lost.'

"So that's what they did, and Beau ran around and around the pond, taking lots of flying leaps into the air. But he still couldn't get off the ground, even with those goose feathers sticking out all over him.

"'Oh, woe, we've got a big problem,' said the bigger goose. 'We can't just leave you here now that you know the secret! No offense, but we sort of don't trust you to keep it.'"

I pause and look down at Freddy to see if that means anything to him personally. It doesn't seem to.

"'Here's what we'll do,' continued the medium-size goose. 'We geese will hold the ends of this pickapoo branch in our bills, and you will bite the middle. We will flap our feathers. You will flap your four strong, muscular legs. Together, we will fly!'

"'Good idea. But remember,' said the bigger goose. 'Don't tell anyone where we are going!'

"'I've told you before, and I'll tell you again,' said Beau. 'I can keep a secret! Especially if you are asking me over and over and over not to share it! Let's leave right away!'

"So the geese bit the ends of the pickapoo branch and Beau bit the middle. He bit it so hard, his teeth were shaky and black for the rest of his future lives. And away they went, up, up, into the sky. Everyone flapped, and that's the way they flew.

"Way down below in the Eastern Rebusinian pastures, the cows mooed, 'Hey, you up there! Where are you going?'

"But Beau and the geese just kept on flapping and didn't say a word.

"By and by, they were flying higher than the pickapoo groves where the birds made their nests.

"'Where are you going?' chirped the birds.

"But Beau and the geese kept on flapping and didn't tell their secret.

"'Where are you going?' brayed a family of donkeys, trudging along a dusty road.

"Beau and the geese kept on flapping and didn't answer. Beau was so proud of himself! *Now the geese know how well I can keep a secret!* he thought.

"Suddenly, the smallest donkey brayed, 'HOO-HAH! HOO's that funny-looking goose in the middle, the one with the feathers sticking out all over?'

"Beau, who as you know was very vain, opened his mouth

to say, 'I am not a funny-looking goose! It's me, me, ME, Beau! The handsomest cat in Eastern Rebusina! And Western Rebusina, too, once we get there!'

"He opened his mouth to say all that, and, of course, let go of the pickapoo branch. The only thing he did get to say was 'EE-OW! EE-OWEY! I'M FALLING!' as he fell down, down, down to the ground."

I pause again, dramatically.

"Then, SPLAT!

"And that was the end of Beau, as we know him."

I know it's a gruesome ending, but Splat's the only ending there could be. My father told me that about stories: If the ending fits, then keep it.

Still, I am worried about how Fred will take it.

But Fred takes it very well.

"EE-OW! EE-OWEY! I'm falling!" he says, hanging over the edge of the bed.

"The story didn't scare you?" I ask.

"No. Because it's to be continued, right?" he asks.

"Oh, right," I say. "And the story continues in Oakland, because the map of Western Rebusina looked like northern California and the geese were all mixed up."

"Cool," says Freddy, still upside down.

"And the moral of the story is . . . ?"

"What's a moral?" asks Fred.

"Something you learn from hearing a story."

"Oh, OK. Never try to fly unless you were born with feathers," says Fred.

I laugh. "Go back to bed," I say.

Actually, I'm not sure what the moral of the story is. I'm not even sure it's about secrets. Maybe it's "Don't be too vain." But I wish Zook were still vain, bathing himself all over with his tongue, the way he used to.

I remember asking my father, "Is that a true story?" I'd never heard of pickapoo groves and yaba-blabba birds, so I was a bit suspicious.

My father said, "Well, I'm not sure it really happened. But let's call it truly a story."

Truly a funny story. I feel a lot better, now that I've told it. And I'm not angry at Freddy anymore. Actually, I'm thinking he didn't really spill the beans about the money in my underwear drawer, because he probably thought Mom knew all about it already. Five-year-olds think moms can read minds—ever notice?

16

I AM DREAMING

I am dreaming about a cat's purr.

A cat's purr is beautiful, like a strange lullaby.

Prrrrrrr . . . Prrrrrrr . . .

A cat's purr feels like a car's motor running.

A cat's purr has a smell, too, of kibble and litter and rain and sun and all the people who love it.

And if I could taste a purr, I bet it would taste like taffy. Or the maple syrup on my pancakes for breakfast.

I'm thinking all this in my dream. I'm hungry for syrup on pancakes, so I make a dream decision. I decide to wake up. You can sometimes do that while you're sleeping—ever notice?

Except now that I'm awake, I still hear that purring. I feel something warm and heavy lying across my legs. I open my eyes, lift my head, and take a peek.

And there's Zook! A real-life Zook, stretching his big brown limbs and looking straight at me with his denim-blue eyes! I am not dreaming. At least, I don't think so. I pinch my arm like you're supposed to do when you're checking those things out. The pinch hurts.

I am not dreaming.

I begin to cry tears of joy. These are my first tears of joy ever. Three seconds ago, I didn't believe in tears of joy. But what do you know? Here they are.

Zook meows, then pulls himself up and lumbers over to me across the blankets. He licks my tears of joy. I draw my blanket over both of us. He still has that alcohol-banana smell from the vet.

"Welcome home, big Zook," I say.

Now my mother comes into the bedroom, my brother Freddy behind her. "We were waiting for both of you to wake up!" Fred says. He jumps onto my bed and crawls under the blanket with me and Zook.

"You have your shoes on," I say.

"Oh, I forgot," says Freddy, kicking them off under the covers.

"Zook was lying outside your bedroom all night, waiting to come in," my mother says. And she lies down beside me, her arm around both me and Fred, a pretty full lower bunk. My mom and I are looking into each other's eyes. She smells so good. She looks happy again. I'm glad.

"I'm thinking about—" I say. My mother hugs me.

"I know," she says.

I'm thinking about that time in the hospital with my mom and me in the bed with my father and the wicker basket and the napkin with strawberries on it, and the same alcohol-banana smell, and Zook purring so loud, just like now. Just like that other time, I have to get up to pee. But now I don't want to think about that other time anymore, because today is a Beau Soleil happy day. Zook is home.

So I get up and go to the bathroom and then I blow my nose. When I come back, my mother is still lying with Zook, and she has a certain Look on her face. A kind of scrunched up Look that means she has to say some hard things.

"What?" I ask.

"Three things," she says. "Actually, four things. Number one: This was Dylan's doing, you know."

"What do you mean?"

"He's a nurse, Oona, and feels very comfortable using

a needle to give subcutaneous fluids. *Subcutaneous* means 'under the skin.' He's going to help us care for Zook at home. He really wants to do that. And Oona, I like him." She touches my cheek, and her own cheeks are pink. "I know he came into our lives all of a sudden. But you'll like him, too. I know you will. So no more name-calling. Please, Oona."

I open my mouth to say something. I guess I leave it open too long, looking for the right words to keep my mom so happy. But my mother is already moving on.

"Two: No more dancing at O'Leary's. I've already spoken to them."

I nod dully. I was kind of expecting that.

"Three: Dylan will be picking up Fred from now on."

"On his bike?" I say. Freddy whoops with excitement and does a somersault on the bed.

"He has a car," says my mother. "Actually, a truck." Freddy whoops again, just a bit less excitedly. He likes trucks, as do I. I really think pickups are cool, except that's way beside the point. But there's no time to plead my case, because my mom is on to Number Four.

"And four: I'm forbidding you to wear that Raiders sweat-shirt anymore."

"No way," I say. I wiggle away from my mother and sit up.

"Way," says my mother, trying to be cool.

"But it smells like Daddy," I cry out.

"Oona, it doesn't smell like anyone but you. It doesn't get laundered enough to smell of anything else. It stinks, frankly. OK, OK, I don't mean that exactly." My mother looks guilty, as if she's just called me a bad name. "But it smells like pizza and the alley, and our own kitchen, and all the places Oona Armstrong hangs out. Not bad smells, but not the odors you want on something you wear. Every day."

"STINKS!" agrees Freddy, snuggling contentedly against Zook.

I walk over to the sweatshirt, flung on a chair. I pick it up and bury my nose in it. Dad. Sugarless gum and pine needle soap. Fainter and fainter, maybe just a memory. But still him.

"It doesn't smell bad," I say. "Those are your own subjective opinions." I've always wanted a chance to say that, ever since I found out what *subjective* means. "Mom, I think we should agree to disagree about this," I add.

And "agree to disagree" is one of the maturest things a person can say.

"We can agree to disagree all you want, but you're still not wearing that sweatshirt anymore." My mother is sitting up now, and her mouth is that angry, straight line, which means "over her dead body," which would make Freddy and me orphans. I can't win.

"Well, I'm going to stay in my bedroom forever then," I say. I can hear how babyish I sound.

Actually, for about ten seconds, I really mean it. I will be Autodidact Kid in my Raiders sweatshirt. I will stay in my room and learn everything I need online all by myself. And I'm sure I can convince Gramma Dee to sneak in tons of books, too, along with my meals. Gramma Dee loves sharing books and discussing them. She and Soma attend two book groups together.

During these ten seconds, out of the corner of my eye, I can see Zook pulling himself up and moving toward the end of my bunk. My mother and I are still staring each other down, and I'm thinking my Autodidact Kid thoughts. Only Freddy notices Zook climbing onto the chair.

"Look!" he says.

Zook is standing on top of my sweatshirt, and he's kneading it back and forth, back and forth, with his big front paws. That's what cats do when they're sleepy and about to hunker down for a snooze. It's instinctive, going back to when they were kittens drinking their mama's milk. I myself get a warm milk feeling inside me, watching Zook do that.

"Everything's settled, then," says my mother. "Looks like your sweatshirt is now officially a cat bed. At least Zook likes that smell." She gives me a quick look.

I duck my head, trying hard to hide my smile.

"Hey, saw that smile!" my mother says.

There's an old, old custom in my family. It began way back before I was born, when my parents were first married. If there's an argument going on and one of the arguers smiles, then the argument's over and a compromise must be reached.

"All right," says my mother. "A compromise must be reached. You can wear that sweatshirt once a month. Take the deal or leave it. Now get dressed. Dylan's coming over to begin Zook's home treatment. And no black. I'm tired of seeing you in that color."

"Black's not a color," I say.

"Right. Then I rest my case."

I shrug one shoulder, but we both know I've given in. I'm not ready to be an autodidact. Yet.

Anyway, Zook's home. Zook's home! And he likes his new bed. Will I want to wear Zook's bed, even if it's only once a month? I don't think so. But I don't admit that to my mom.

I've grown in the past few months since I began wearing

that sweatshirt full-time. All my tops are too tight, except for one T-shirt that Maria and Mario gave me. Men's size small, with O'LEARY'S—PIZZA SUPREMO on the back. It used to be way, way too big, but now it's just a bit too big. So that's what I wear.

17

FIDDLE-I-FEE

Now I will see Zook and the Villain, together at last! I will be watching his every move, prepared to point out the clues of his villainry to my mom. I'm just sorry I have to be the one to do that to her.

The Villain comes over carrying a cardboard box. He removes some scary-looking things, spreading them all out on the coffee table in the living room: a long, snakelike, see-through tube, a needle that looks like a little weapon, and a coat hanger. He takes out a paper pouch, tears it open, and removes a clear bag filled with something that looks like water. He puts that bag into our salad bowl, which Mom has filled with warm water.

"We're going to warm up this fluid solution and then get

it under Zook's skin," he says. "Think of it like the Gatorade athletes drink when they're dehydrated. The solution is made up of some good stuff: sodium and potassium and calcium, which Zook needs."

"Yum," I say.

The Villain dries off the bag. Then he attaches one end of the long tube, called a drip line, to the bottom of the bag. He attaches a needle to the other end of the drip line. He pushes the hooked part of the coat hanger through the top of the bag and hooks it to our living room bookshelf.

"Look at Dylan's hands," says Gramma Dee. "Beautiful hands, like the hands of God painted on the ceiling of the Sistine Chapel."

When Gramma Dee says that, the Villain laughs. "Not quite," he says.

"What's the Sistine Chapel?" I ask.

"The Sistine Chapel is a famous chapel in Vatican City, which is a tiny country inside of Italy," Gramma Dee says.

Gramma Dee is always going on about the trip to Italy and India she's going to take with Soma one of these days, when they've retired and saved up enough funds. Gramma Dee pulls an art book from our shelf to show us this special ceiling. Sure enough, there's God, with wavy hair, a long gray beard, and muscles, kindly stretching out his big hand to give life to a tired-looking Adam. It was painted by a famous artist named Michelangelo way back in the 1500s.

My mom giggles. "I think you're being overly dramatic, Ma," she says.

"No, I'm not," says Gramma Dee, looking at the painting and then at Dylan. "Those are healing hands, and that makes them beautiful."

I look at the Villain's hands. His fingers are slender and brown. They look like ordinary hands to me, except for the long nails on his right hand for all that guitar-plucking. I watch them suspiciously.

"Bring on the patient," the Villain says.

My mother brings Zook from our bedroom, where he's been snoozing. He's wrapped up in my Raiders sweatshirt and only his head peeps out.

"I've wrapped him up in case he protests," she says.

"What do you mean?" I ask.

"Honey, Dylan will be injecting him," my mother says.

I knew that. On the other hand, I didn't. You can know and not know something at the very same time—ever notice?

I glance at the Villain for some sign that he recognizes Zook. Of course, he's already seen Zook because he and my mom picked him up from the vet last night. So he's had plenty of time to compose himself.

Right now, the Villain's all business. "Let's begin," he says.

Beside our living room bookshelf is this giant tattered chair covered in brown corduroy that can easily hold two people, maybe three if two of the people aren't that big. It's always been a TV chair and a scratching post for Zook. But now it's turned into a kind of hospital chair. Zook's in my lap, lying on my sweatshirt. I'm sitting close to the chair's arm, which is like a barricade, so Zook can't squirm away. The Villain is squeezed beside me, and Freddy beside him.

The Villain whispers, "Good boy, good boy" as he's petting Zook. Then suddenly, he reaches over and lifts up the scruff of Zook's coat between Zook's shoulder blades. With his other hand, he jabs in the needle.

"EE-OWEY!" howls Zook.

Fred and I jump.

"Doesn't hurt him," says the Villain calmly.

"Yeah, sure," I say. "Maybe he doesn't need any more fluids, now that he's home with us. He's been doing OK today."

The Villain takes my hand so I can feel where the needle is. He puts his hand over mine. "See? It's just Zook's coat, not his flesh. Now, keep your hand on the needle so it doesn't get pulled out."

"How long's this going to take?" my mother asks.

"About ten minutes," says the Villain.

"We'll go make the pancakes," says my mom. She and Gramma Dee leave the three of us sitting in the chair.

"Now watch the fluid in the bag," the Villain says. "It will slowly go down as the fluid drips through the tubing into Zook." He points to a line on the bag. "When the fluid gets to this line, he's had enough." He pushes a little wheel on a small box attached to the tubing, and I see the fluid slowly begin to go down.

The Villain still has his hand over mine because Zook is squirming. He begins to sing a really dumb song in his soft Marvin Gaye voice, over and over.

I bought me a cat and the cat pleased me.
I fed my cat under yonder tree.
Cat goes fiddle-i-fee, fiddle-i-fee.

Freddy starts singing that dumb song with him. I'm sure he doesn't even know what "yonder" means, but Freddy doesn't care. Soon Zook stops squirming.

"How's it going?" Gramma Dee pokes her head out from the kitchen.

"Good," says the Villain. "We're almost done." We watch the bag. The Villain's hand over mine is warm. He smells like coffee.

"Oona, listen to me," says the Villain quietly. "I give you my word. This will help Zook. I promise."

His promise feels like a gift. Sitting beside the Villain, his warm hand over mine, I want to believe him so much! I stop thinking about clues of villainry and anyway, I can't find any at this moment. Even if the Villain is the greatest actor in the world, I don't care. All I want is Zook to feel better. I even start singing that dumb song, too.

When the fluid gets to the line, the Villain lifts my hand and pries the needle from Zook's coat. "There," he says.

I once saw a TV show where a doctor cured a baby by opening up her chest to get to her heart, a procedure no one in the world had ever done before. It was a long time ago, in the 1940s. The baby's lips were blue because there was a blockage somewhere and her blood didn't have enough oxygen in it. So the doctor stitched one of her heart arteries to another artery. That way blood with enough oxygen in it could get to her lungs. Suddenly, the baby's face glowed, her lips and cheeks pink and healthy-looking! Really, it was like a miracle. Everyone in the TV operating room cheered, and so did I. I will never forget that show.

I'm not saying Zook's procedure is just as dramatic, because first of all, that was a television show and they used all those special effects and everything. And second of all, this is not the first time in the world anyone has ever given a cat fluids. Still, it feels dramatic. Zook jumps off my lap, looking perkier than he's looked in quite a while. Fit as a fiddle, actually.

"Breakfast's ready," calls my mom.

The pancakes smell good.

"This stuff expensive?" I ask, pointing to the big cardboard box filled with more bags of fluid and tubing.

The Villain shrugs.

"How about I contribute my dancing money?" I say. I'm thinking that what we have here is our very own cat rescue society.

The Villain smiles, shaking his head no.

"Great idea!" yells my mom from the kitchen.

That's another weird talent of my mom's: hearing things through walls when I'm on the other side.

* 18 *

GALILEO AND THE THEORY OF NOTICING

Today, just as we get to the schoolyard, I notice that Riya is wearing one green sock and one purple-and-pink striped sock. Riya is very careful about what she wears, so I don't think this is a mistake. I myself am wearing two white socks. It's the only color my mom buys for us because it's easy to make a pair again if one sock is swallowed up by our building's washing machine. My mom says that every new washing machine comes with two things: a free box of soap and a monster deep down in the machine's bowels with a huge craving for smelly socks. Yum.

White socks happen to match my O'Leary's shirt—not that I care that much about matching.

"I think what you did at the vet took a lot of *chutzpah*," says Riya.

Riya has complimented me before on my *chutzpah*, which means "nerve." She learned the Yiddish word from her grandmother, who learned it from Gramma Dee.

The thing is, I haven't told her anything about what happened at the vet.

"Wait a minute. How do you know what I did at the vet?" I ask. "I wanted to keep that story private for a while." Because I'm still pondering a few things. Why exactly I did it, for instance.

"Oh," says Riya. She gives me a quick look, guilty around the edges. Then she looks down at her socks. "Wasn't it you who told me? Oh. Right. It was my *didu*."

Which, I guess, is another thing her grandmother learned from Gramma Dee.

There's a little cluster of kids by the basketball net, as always, doing layups. The first thing I notice is that most of them are wearing socks that don't match, even some of the boys.

Riya notices me noticing. "Over the weekend a few of us decided to start a fad," she explains. "We want to see how fast it will catch on throughout the whole school. Maybe the whole city!" Then she adds quickly, tossing her hair, "I didn't think you'd be interested."

She's right, of course. A girl who wears a Raiders sweatshirt all the time, moving on to an O'Leary's T-shirt only a few days ago, isn't going to be thinking about her socks. Anyway, it's a dumb fad. A done-before, ho-hum, no-point fad.

Still, I would have liked a chance to say no.

Leo calls out, "Hey, Oona! 'Napped any cats lately?" His left sock is white, the right one blue with yellow peace signs all over it, which I'm guessing he borrowed from one of his parents.

Somebody else says (I can't tell who because I'm looking at Riya who is NOT looking at me), "Pizza delivery? Over here!"

I was going to yell out something red-whoppery, such as needing to go straight to work at O'Leary's in my uniform right after school. But then I figured, why even bother responding to immaturity? There was more snickering all around about cat-napping, etc., etc. Of course they heard it through the grapevine, just like in that song. Phonevine, actually, and textvine, and e-vine, stretching from Gramma Dee to Soma to Riya and beyond.

I walk away. I vow NEVER to speak to Riya again.

This morning the Rowdies, who include most of the sock people, are in fine form. They're talking, shuffling their feet, looking inside their desks for stuff. I try to concentrate because Mr. Fry, as usual, has something interesting to say. He is talking about a Theory of Noticing, although he doesn't call it a theory, exactly.

"Galileo saw things that made him believe that the Earth orbits around the Sun, rather than the other way around," Mr. Fry says. "Even when people arrested him and made him take that theory back, he still said, 'But it moves!'"

Somebody in the back of the room burps, and it could have been a not-on-purpose burp, but of course that burp is the funniest thing the Rowdies have ever heard.

"And scientists have long noticed that the east coast of South America seems to fit together with the west coast of Africa, like a giant jigsaw puzzle that someone broke up. And other scientists thought that theory was absolutely ridiculous. 'Continents drifting apart,' they said, 'ha, ha!'"

"Ha, ha, ha! Hee, hee, hee! Ho, ho, ho!" go the Rowdies under their breaths.

"That's how great thinkers come up with theories," Mr. Fry continues. "They observe things, but they don't always observe the same things others do, especially when others are observing the obvious, but wrong, things. And I hope that you youngsters are creative in your observations, too."

Jigsaw puzzle continents!

I sit up straight in my seat. My mouth falls open, because I have just heard one of the wisest things a teacher has ever said! Except maybe Mr. Fry shouldn't use the word "youngsters." That always sets off the Rowdies.

I look around to see if everyone else is as excited about Mr. Fry's Noticing-the-Obvious-but-Wrong-Things Theory. Nobody is, as far as I can see. They're talking to one another or *hee-hee-hee*ing or, because it's almost recess, staring up at the clock. I feel bad for Mr. Fry with his kind, kind eyes and wet hair. To my surprise, tears roll out of my own eyes, and then a whole lot of really loud caps roll out of my mouth.

"EVERYBODY PIPE DOWN!" I shout. "PLEASE!"

There is a stunned silence, and things do quiet down a bit, especially when Riya says, "Yeah!" from across the room. I look over at her and we have an eye-conversation, the kind that usually happens between siblings or true loves or meant-to-be-cousins. Her eyes say, *Hey, I get it*. My eyes say, *Thank you, best friend of mine. I'm not angry at you anymore.* And then the bell rings.

During recess, Mr. Fry and I have another ten-minute father figure session.

"Well," says Mr. Fry, shutting the classroom door. He sits on his desk, pulling himself up with a little grunt.

He doesn't really have to do that for me, sit on his desk and look so scrunched up and uncomfortable, trying to be friendly and cool. In my mind Mr. Fry is already nice, even if he's not cool. I do notice that one of his socks is blue and the other sock is black, although in his case it was probably because of bad lighting when he got dressed. I'm positive he wasn't part of that dumb fad grapevine.

"Well," says Mr. Fry again. "Thank you for that intervention. Feeling better?"

I wasn't expecting a thank-you! I nod my head. "I just wanted everyone to hear the wise things you were saying."

"Well. You were quite dramatic, I must say," says Mr. Fry, and he grins. Mr. Fry is handsome when he grins, which isn't very often. He smiles, but that's a whole different thing from grinning—ever notice?

Mr. Fry isn't wearing a wedding ring. Some married people don't. "Mr. Fry, are you married?" I ask.

Mr. Fry blushes faintly. "No," he says. "Not yet."

It sounds like he already has someone in his life, and I am glad for him. "I was just curious," I say.

"Well," says Mr. Fry.

After a while, the school bell rings. Mr. Fry slides off the desk and says, "By the way, I like your shirt. I haven't had O'Leary's pizza myself yet. Supremo, eh?"

"I highly recommend it," I say.

Riya and I walk home together after school.

"I was hoping that my mom and Mr. Fry would go out for tea sometime," I say. "But now I think it would be weird for my mom to be good friends with my teacher."

This time Riya doesn't want to ignore our fight from that morning. Her words burst out all in a rush, not in caps, but bent over in italics, as if she's been holding them in too long. *"Oona I'm sorry I told what you did at the vet and I'm sorry I didn't include you in that sock thing but of course socks aren't as important as Zook!"*

"Apology accepted," I say.

She isn't finished. Her words in italics pour out even faster. *"And Oona no offense but I was beginning to think YOU were weird wearing that sweatshirt all the time! I know it was in honor of your father and that took a lot of* chutzpah *wearing it no matter what. But really you've been sort of weird no offense and now I bet you're going to be wearing that oversize O'Leary's thing every day!"*

"Well, my sweatshirt's a cat bed now, and none of my other tops fit me," I say, frowning, and yes, taking offense.

Riya stops walking. "A cat bed?" she says.

"Zook's," I say.

I snort. Riya snorts. Then we're laughing our heads off, shrieking and snorting and not caring who hears.

"Hey, I can lend you some tops if you like," Riya says, catching her breath after a while. "We're the same size now."

I look over at Riya. I hadn't noticed, but yes, we're the same size. Riya used to be the smaller one! Everything's changing. Continents are drifting and new stars are forming and my sweatshirt's a cat bed.

"OK," I say.

✶ 19

MY COMMON-LETTER-OF-THE-ALPHABET THEORY

If sunshine were called prune juice, it would still be sunshine. Words are just words—ever notice? The word "villain" doesn't have as evil a meaning to me anymore.

But still, I am trying to think of the Villain as Dylan now. That way "Villain" doesn't pop out of my mouth and cause a big uproar. It's hard, but a lot of the time, it's not.

On this sunshiny Saturday, our family is invited to see what Dylan has done to his backyard.

I am finishing up my breakfast with Gramma Dee. She's a vegetarian, but her big exception is smoked fish, and she's brought some over. We're the only ones who love smoked fish in our family. My mother says it's too smelly, and Fred's scared of that fish with its surprised googly eyes lying there on the plate. And that's fine with me. Because when Gramma Dee and I eat smoked fish together for breakfast, we usually have a nice heart-to-heart.

Gramma Dee wipes her mouth. She has something on her mind, I can tell, and she's taking her time looking for the right words. She leans close to me and says, "Between you and me, Dylan's a little *meshuga*, in my humble opinion."

I almost choke on my fish. "What?" I say.

Meshuga is another Yiddish word. It means "crazy." And when Gramma Dee says "in my humble opinion," she doesn't really mean that. She means just the opposite, like "smart" or "terrific" opinion. Believe me, she wouldn't give her opinion if she thought it were wrong.

"He and Soma and their gardens! Your mom calls them 'urban farmers'! But who needs to grow their own vegetables and fruits and herbs in this day and age? My great-grandparents grew their own food, but that was in the old country. OK, it was mostly potatoes. But they were farmers. They didn't have a perfectly modern Whole Foods and a Safeway within driving distance."

My mom comes into the kitchen. "Keep an open mind, Ma," she says. "Wait until you see it."

"Urban farmer! That young man's beautiful hands are for music and healing," says Gramma Dee. "Not for digging in the dirt."

Right then and there is when I come up with my Common-Letter-of-the-Alphabet Theory.

There are three important things about Dylan, and they all begin with the same letter: the letter *H*.

1. Dylan is a nurse. He HEALS.
2. Dylan's HANDS are strong, but gentle, like the hands Michelangelo drew on the ceiling of the Sistine Chapel.
3. Dylan makes my mother HAPPY.

That has to mean something, right? Is it possible for a three-H person, a healing nurse with Michelangelo hands who makes my mom happy, to abuse a cat?

Maybe. Maybe not.

Is it possible I was noticing the obvious but wrong things, like all those long-ago great thinkers used to do, the ones who were very wise, but very, very mistaken about the Earth and the Sun and the continents?

Maybe. Maybe not.

A street address on a cat's collar. A pirate's braid. A name that rhymes with villain. Obvious but wrong clues of villainry? I don't know. I haven't had much experience with villains. But I'm beginning to think that my Name Theory isn't all that great a theory.

There is one possible way to find out the truth.

My mother and my grandmother think taking Zook with us to Dylan's backyard is a crazy idea.

"No, Oona," my mother says. "Zook's been an indoor cat for too long now."

"Well, I think it's a good idea," I say.

Dylan has come over to give Zook his morning fluids. When he hears my plan, he takes my side. "Why not?" he asks. "The sun will be good for him."

Of course he has just said my two favorite words. Well, my two favorite words when they are standing right next to each other. And Dylan sure doesn't sound like someone with something to hide.

"Yes, why not?" I ask.

My mom and Gramma Dee are old pros when it comes to answering that question.

"He's old," says my mom.

"And he has a condition," says Gramma Dee.

"Also, he may run away," my mom points out.

We look over at Zook, and we all laugh. Zook is lying on his back on the braided kitchen rug. His legs are splayed comfortably, his fat belly facing the sun that is streaming through the window. He's waving one paw, trying to capture a floating speck of fluff. Zook looks like a hairy sunbather at the beach.

"I don't think he'll run away, in my humble opinion," I say.

So off we go, with Zook in his carrier.

We enter Dylan's backyard through the driveway. The backyard is a blaze of sunshine and smoke. I blink as I enter. It is so sunny, everything looks yellow and white at first. Then, as my eyes get used to the sunshine, I see amazing colors, like crazy paint poured all over the place. Blobs of red, swirly swoops of yellow, a jumble of orange and purple. And great big splashes of cool green in between.

Mario and Maria are barbecuing pizza dough on a grill.

"Dylan's our newest zucchini supplier!" says Mario. "Who knows? We may start using other vegetables at O'Leary's."

"It's about time, Mr. Creature of Habit," says Maria.

That surprises me, because I'd always thought that Mario and Maria agreed on everything, especially the wonderfulness of fried zook!

Dylan is grinning. He looks proud of his garden, and there

are a hundred reasons to be proud, believe you me. "Let me give you a tour," he says.

The garden is small, but its paths meander and circle. We walk around and around, and the garden seems to grow bigger as we walk. Plants are everywhere, in pots, in big dirt-filled boxes, and in the ground. Dylan gives all the amazing colors their vegetable names. Early Girl tomatoes and little pale orangey-green Sun Gold ones. Scarlet runner beans. Green zucchini with yellow blossoms. Furry green beans winding around his chain-link fence. Plump strawberries like polka dots, and the big purple flowers of an artichoke plant. And herbs (urbs!) everywhere: mint and basil and thyme, and others, lots of others, except I can't remember all their names.

"I have plants from all over the place," Dylan says. "Here are California natives, poppies and goldenrod, growing in the sun near a Japanese maple and New Zealand flax."

A multi-culty garden! I don't have to imagine a faraway magical forest, that game I always play in Soma's garden. Dylan's garden is magical already. And I don't want to be anywhere else but right here.

Zook flops down and lolls around, doing his hairy sun-bather act. Every now and then he gets up to smell or nibble.

I am watching him carefully. No, I can't say he recognizes where he is, but he sure looks happy.

Soon we're also lolling around, on garden chairs that Dylan has brought out. Our stomachs are stuffed with barbecued pizza and fried veggies and ricotta cake and cold mint tea.

"OK, I like this garden," admits Gramma Dee, kicking off her sandals and wriggling her toes. "My mind has been opened. So, Dylan, where did you learn to do all this?"

I'm staring at the purple artichoke flowers, happy to learn that an ugly duckling vegetable like an artichoke can blossom into something so beautiful. The purple of its flower makes me dizzy, but in a sleepy, happy way. I burp softly; I can't help it. Beside me, Freddy laughs. Rowdies and five-year-olds think burps are the funniest things—ever notice?

Dylan is talking about an old, old man, some relative of his. I'm not really listening at first.

". . . my great-uncle Phineas, the coolest, kindest guy on the planet. Phin for short. I was like a grandson to him because he had no children of his own. I came to live with him when my parents died. He taught me the guitar. And he taught me everything I know about growing things. He put in all the trees here and a lot of the raised beds himself. I just added a few more, pruned a lot, weeded a lot, and beefed up the soil a bit."

Now I'm sitting up. I'm not dizzy anymore. My mind is as sharp as a rose thorn.

"Phin wrote me letters when I was traveling around on my bike, working in different cities. I always made sure he knew where I was, and he always made sure to write. About this garden, or a book he was reading, or his spinach and dumpling soup. Or his cat."

"His cat," I say hoarsely. I look over at Zook, who is drinking from a leaky faucet at the side of the house, where a hose is attached. And now I'm waiting. I'm waiting for the story I've begun to hope for. The story I knew, deep-down, was there all along.

"Yup. He had this old cat he'd picked up at the pound for company. Phin was lonely when I was gone, I guess. 'We're two old cats, just hangin' and howlin' together!' Phin wrote me." Dylan stares down at his hands as if Phin's letter were right there. Then he shakes his head and looks up at the beautiful garden. "Oh, man, he loved that animal!"

Zook is rolling around on a gravel path, scratching his back. Then he lumbers over to one of the raised beds, climbs in, and rolls around some more.

"Will you look at that?" Dylan points to Zook. "Cats are all the same! Phin said his cat used to roll around in the garden dirt like that, too. In fact, his name was—"

Mud.

"—Mud. Saddest thing, though. Phin moved and took Mud with him, but one day Mud just jumped out an open window and disappeared."

Open window. Miraculo. Jewel.

Now Dylan reaches for his guitar beside the lounge chair. "I think this calls for some Muddy Waters," he says.

"What's Muddy Waters?" Gramma Dee asks.

Dylan opens his eyes wide, as if he just can't believe Gramma Dee asked that question. "Whoa. You don't know who Muddy Waters is?" he asks. "Muddy Waters was a famous blues singer. He sang the blues and he lived them. So did Phin. And that cat, Mud, did, too. Muddy was another reason for Mud's name, because that cat could sure sing. At least, that's what Phin said. OK, listen here."

Dylan picks up his guitar, looks straight at my mom, and sings.

Baby, please don't go,
Baby, please don't go,

Baby, please don't go down to New Orleans,
You know I love you so.

I'm sitting here thinking I'm going to tell them the truth, right now. But there's my mother smiling with her whole body, and you know she's not going to New Orleans. She's not going anywhere, because she's staying right here in this happy garden. And Dylan sings another song about mojo and another about something called hoochie coochie and another about rollin' stones, and they are songs that are sad and happy at the same time, the saddest and happiest songs I've ever heard. You wouldn't think that's possible, but it is. And my mother's still smiling at him, happy, happy, happy. I'm going to tell them the truth. After this song. No, after this song. No, after this next song, for sure.

Then: "EE-OW! EE-OWEY!"

I don't have to tell anybody anything, because here's Zook, doing it for me. Zook, singing the blues with Dylan.

Dylan stops his playing. Zook stops singing. Dylan strums a few chords, like a soft, low growl. "Ee-ow! Ee-owey!" sings Zook, softly and growly, too. Dylan's long nails pluck a loud whine; his left hand whizzes up and down the neck of the guitar. "EE-OW! EE-OWEY!" howls Zook, not missing a beat.

Dylan lays down his guitar, and Zook is quiet, too. But the music and Zook's song are still humming in my ears. Now Zook's rubbing up against Dylan's leg as if he owns him, and all of us are quiet, staring at that cat. Dylan leans over and scoops up Zook.

"Another thing about Mud," Dylan says softly. He holds one of Zook's paws in his big Michelangelo hand. "He had twenty-six toes, Phin told me. That's very, very rare. Most cats have only eighteen."

Dylan picks up each of Zook's paws, one after the other. We are all silently counting, even though everyone, except Dylan, already knows the total.

"It's him," whispers my mother. "I've told you how Oona and Fred found Zook." But she tells the story again about that sunny Saturday, about finding our cat, Phin's cat, stretched out in a pot of geraniums. Then she reaches for Dylan's hand and she kisses Dylan's fingers, one by one.

"Oh, my, oh, my," says Gramma Dee.

Maria and Mario are shouting something in another

language, which I'm guessing means WOW in either Italian or Spanish.

So there you go. It's like when you're lying on the floor doing a jigsaw puzzle and there are only a couple of pieces left and you know where they belong, easy. You snap them into their places, all the curvy parts and the angles and the corners fitting together exactly the way they should. Snap. Snap. Snap.

Except this is a real-life jigsaw puzzle, with all the missing pieces in place. Life isn't usually like that, but today it is.

"THAT IS SO ROMANTIC!" yells Riya when I tell her on the phone. "You found Zook, and because of that your Gramma Dee met my *didu*, and because of that your mother met Uncle Dylan, and now Zook has found more loved ones. A happy ending! It's *karma*!"

"I guess," I say.

I don't understand *karma* very well. Riya says nobody except incredibly wise people do, but it's something about past lives and present lives and future lives and how they are connected somehow, and how nothing in our lives happens accidentally. It's very complicated and there are big books written about it.

The truth is, it was all because of my yellow whopper, not *karma*. And that sure spoils the happy ending, like a big splotch of mustard on a clean cloth napkin.

Because I didn't find Zook.

I stole him.

20

Life Number Four

MUD

Dylan is teaching us a few things. He and Freddy have a little rosemary garden growing in one of the big blue alley pots. And Dylan's teaching me and Freddy how to give Zook his fluids. We sit in our hospital chair with Zook between us. Freddy grabs the fur of Zook's neck and holds it tightly. Dylan guides my hand as I jab the needle in. I do it gently but firmly, just like Dylan tells me to, and Zook doesn't even flinch. Freddy announces he's going to be a doctor or a nurse or a vet when he grows up; maybe he'll be all three. My mother and Dylan grin at each other because Freddy sounds so cute when he says that. But honestly, I was thinking the same thing myself. Those jobs are possibilities for both of us.

We unhook Zook from his needle and my mom takes him into her arms. We all stand around, stroking Zook's damp fur. "Oh, Zook," says my mom, bending her head to nuzzle the top of his head. "Do you think he minds if we call him Zook instead of Mud?"

"Of course he doesn't mind!" says Fred. "That's his name now. Mud's the name from another story."

My mother looks up. "Another story?"

"I've been teaching Freddy how to read by telling him cat stories," I say quickly. "I'm using rebuses."

"Rebuses!" says my mom. "I'd forgotten about those. That's how Oona's father taught her to read," she explains to Dylan.

"I'll be right back," Freddy says. He runs into our bedroom and returns with some paper and his crayon box. "*I'm* going to tell this story. I'm going to make some rebuses, too."

Freddy sits on the floor with the paper and crayons in front of him. He pulls his left ear, his story ear, and begins.

"Well, a cat landed SPLAT, and when he got up again, he still had all those toes and that diamond, but now he had brown fur.

"'EE-OWEY! Where am I?' he meowed.

"He was lying on his back, so he looked down at his belly

and there was some white fur in the shape of California, and some black hair where our city, Oakland, is. 'Oh, Oakland. Cool,' said that cat. 'I've always wanted to go there.'

"So he wandered and he wandered, but too bad, the pound man found him and put him in a cage at the city pound, which made that cat so sad. But then one day a lonely old man came to adopt him and that man's name was . . ."

Now Freddy stops to carefully draw a fish with a triangle on one side. He writes "*RW IN*" and points to that triangle.

"Fin," I say. (Some other time I'll tell Freddy that the sound of the letter *F* can sometimes be written *PH*.)

"Good," says Freddy.

"The man's name was Fin. So Fin named that cat Mud because Mud had brown fur, and also he liked to roll around in the mud in Fin's nice backyard. Mud ate fruits and vegetables from the yard and got very, very fat. Fin fed Mud lots of fiddle-i-fee under his tree, and Fin and Mud were happy together. But one day, Fin had to move because his house was falling apart and he needed a new one. He didn't get a chance to put Mud's name and new address on a name tag. Too bad! Because one day Mud jumped out the window just for fun. Cats like to do that. But too bad! Mud was lost because it was a new street and he forgot where he lived.

"So Mud wandered and he wandered and he got skinnier and skinnier. Mud ate hard rolls and bones from garbage cans and that broke some of his teeth. He got into a fight with a wild dog who took a bite out of his ear. And one terrible day . . ."

Fred pauses dramatically. He looks at me and Mom and Dylan, and his eyes get big, and a whole bunch of caps roll out of his mouth: "A GREAT BIG HORRIBLE MEAN TERRIBLE VERY SCARY . . ."

Fred draws a large blue head with green googly eyes and sticking-up black hair and a mouth with yellow jagged teeth, breathing red jaggedy fire. We all stare at it.

"Hmmm . . ." says my mother. "Nothing comes to mind."

"A monster?" Dylan asks.

"Yes!" says Fred. "And monster doesn't rhyme with anything." Then Fred writes BB underneath the monster head.

"Oh, BB-gun monster," I say.

"Of course," Freddy says.

And I'm thinking Freddy's got that exactly right. We'll never, ever know who that monster was, but that's the best name in the world for someone who shoots at cats. Worse than an ordinary villain, in my humble opinion.

Fred continues his story.

"'EE-OW! EE-OWEY! You got me!' meowed Mud. That BB-gun pellet hurt a lot. And he wandered and he wandered some more and went into an alley with garbage pails, where he found some other cats for friends and some leftover pizza, and he felt a little better. Right next to the back of the pizza place was a beautiful, beautiful part of the alley, with big blue pots with lavender and geraniums in them. And there were plenty of fat mice and all the water he needed, dripping from a hose. Now he had everything except people friends to take care of him. And one day he remembered that the diamond on his empty name tag was magic! So he wished upon it! He wished he could see Prince Fredericko and Princess Oonella again, old friends from way, way back. He found something better, because one day, one happy lucky, lucky, lucky day, he found . . ."

Fred draws a rectangle with lots of windows and wheels and a big RW underneath.

"A Recreation Wehicle?" I ask.

"Don't be silly," says Fred. He taps the rectangle a couple of times. "Rhymes with?"

"This is hard," says Dylan.

"Can you give us a hint?" asks my mom.

Fred slowly writes B–U–S, sounding out the letters. Then he puts a big X over the B and shouts, "US, of course!"

"Wow," says my mom. "Great. You have an excellent teacher."

"Prince Fredericko and Princess Oonella! Very imaginative. Good stuff, kid," Dylan says.

Fred looks so proud of his story, I don't even take credit for the prince and the princess part.

Let's say you're doing that jigsaw puzzle and some pieces are missing. Maybe those missing pieces were thrown out with the trash by mistake, or maybe they're in a shadowy corner under your bed that the broom can't reach. It doesn't really matter. You can imagine their shape and color in your mind. After a while, you don't even notice the holes anymore, because what you are imagining feels so right. Fred's just told the pieces of Zook's story I myself should have imagined all along.

All of a sudden, I feel a big, yellow–whoppery lump growing in my belly.

21

F = PH

Phin has been on all our minds.

Well, my mind's been aware of him, but also my belly, because of that big, sour, yellow-whoppery lump inside of it.

We show Dylan Zook's diamond. He holds the pendant in the palm of his hand and rubs the diamond with his thumb.

"Phin wrote me that he'd bought a tag for Mud sporting a diamond. He thought it made Mud look pretty cool, all ready for his new digs. I wish Phin had remembered to put his new info on it. Or maybe he didn't know it yet. But Phin shouldn't have removed the old tag so soon."

But it wasn't Phin who removed the old tag! It was me it was me it was me it was me it was me it was me.

I am afraid to open my mouth in case a giant cartoon bubble floats out with those guilty words swimming around inside of it.

Then Dylan says, "I'd like to arrange a reunion between Zook and Phin, if that's OK. And, of course, I want you all to meet one another, too."

"We'd love that!" says my mother.

I give one of those fake smiles, the kind where you turn up the corners of your mouth but don't open it.

So a few days later we all pile into Mom's car to bring Zook and Phin together again. Zook's in his carrier on Dylan's lap in the front seat.

Dylan's great-uncle didn't really move to a new house. He moved to a Home, the kind with a capital H. It's a Retirement Home. Actually, it has a much fancier name: the Sunrise Assisted Living Facility. They assist you with all the things you may not be able to do anymore when you are very old, like walk, and eat, and dress. And even breathe.

"Just so you know, Phin breathes through an oxygen tank," says Dylan when we reach the Home. "Phin smoked like a fish all his life, and his lungs don't work very well. So the tank gives him air to breathe."

Of course Freddy finds this hilarious, falling down on the

big green lawn of the Home. My mom looks shocked, but I'm not. She doesn't know Fred like I do. Since Dylan came into our lives and my brother's appetite has improved, I'm scared Freddy's turning into one of those Rowdies.

"That's so silly!" yells Freddy. "Fish don't smoke!"

So I explain about smoked fish, like smoked salmon or smoked whitefish, the kind Gramma Dee and I like. I go on and on to Fred about smoked fish. That kind of takes my mind off why we're all here, walking up the great graveled path to the Home, its white stone stairs shining in the sun.

I feel like a villain.

It's not a good feeling. I don't know how other villains feel, but I feel like the lowest of the low, which would be some sort of insect, I guess. I ponder this for a while, dragging my feet up the big stairs. Of course, caterpillars and beetles don't feel like villains, going about their buggy day on the ground.

Then I do some more pondering about the Home's name. How it's Sunrise and not Sunset, because sunrise sounds more hopeful than sunset. But elderly people may not have that many sunrises OR sunsets left. Why remind everybody about all that? Which isn't a good thing to ponder, because then I start pondering about all the sunrises and sunsets Phin and Zook missed together because of villainous me.

We enter the Home. Dylan, carrying Zook, tells a receptionist who we are and she cheerfully chirps, "Phin's so excited to see you!"

We all troop down corridors painted cheerful colors like yellow and pink. Hanging here and there on the walls are cheerful paintings of people wearing old-fashioned clothing, and kids playing with old-fashioned toys like hoops and marbles, so the Sunrise people will think of cheerful things from their past. We meet people pushing walkers, or sitting on benches, or strolling by. Most of them wave or say hi. One lady has a little Chihuahua in her lap, because small pets are allowed here. Cheerfulness is everywhere. I begin to feel a tiny bit more cheerful myself.

Dylan knocks on a door and there is a long silence, the kind of silence that feels like someone's inside, waiting. Dylan holds up a finger as if he's expecting this wait, and after a while we hear a soft voice say, "Come. In."

Phin is sitting in a chair facing the door. You can tell he'd be tall standing up. He's wearing a bright red shirt and shiny black shoes. On his head is one of those nightcaps Mother Goose characters wear to keep their bald heads warm. He's the oldest man I've ever seen, with lines on his face like streets on a map and a bushy gray beard like God on that chapel ceiling. Plastic tubing runs from each of his nostrils and behind his ears. The tubes are attached to a small blue oxygen tank with wheels, sitting on the floor beside his chair. On the other side of his chair is a little table with things laid out for tea, as well as a plate of cookies.

"Hey," Phin says.

Dylan puts down Zook's carrier and introduces us. I notice that even though Phin's body is old, his eyes are young and mischievous. Those eyes stare hard at you, like he could read your mind, which I sincerely hope he can't do. He's probably the kind of person who would make rowdy remarks if he could talk faster. There are little pauses between every word he says.

"Now. Let's. See. My. Guy," Phin says.

Fred opens the carrier and pulls out Zook. Zook's legs dangle over Phin's, and Phin reaches out to take him. Zook gives a little yelp and curls up on Phin's lap.

"Old. Mud," Phin says, stroking Zook, who begins to knead his paws back and forth. Zook is purring and kneading, and Phin is stroking and stroking, and it's as if they just said good-bye only one or two sunrises ago. Then I remember that they didn't really have a chance to say good-bye.

"Still. Rolling. In. The. Mud?" Phin asks.

"Well, we keep him indoors," my mother says. "It's safer that way. There's a lot of traffic where we live, and we don't have a backyard."

Dylan pours tea for everyone, even for Freddy, who puts lots of milk in his and dunks his cookie. Except for Phin, that is, who doesn't let go of Zook, just keeps stroking and stroking him. Mom and Dylan chat with Phin about this and that, and then they explain about giving Zook fluids.

"We're all getting very, very good at it," I say, in case there's a question about whether Zook should come back with us. But soon Phin scoops up Zook and hands him over to me. I put Zook in his carrier right away.

Phin points to a guitar standing in a dark corner. Dylan gives it to him. He kisses Phin's lined cheek. Suddenly, Phin's hands are moving lickety-split over that guitar. There are hardly any spaces between the notes, as if his fingers were doing all the fast talking Phin wished he could do.

"*Ee-ow*," sings Zook softly, tired now.

Phin looks tired, too. He puts aside his guitar and high-fives Freddy and me. Mom and Dylan hug him good-bye, and I pick up Zook's carrier.

Phin leans forward to wiggle a finger through the carrier's cage door.

"We're. Two. Old. Indoor. Cats. Now," he says.

Phin's smiling, but it's sad to think of him and Zook that way. Even though it's true.

We go out into the corridor, and I decide I can't ignore the yellow-whopper lump in my belly anymore. "I'll be right back," I say.

I open Phin's door without knocking, which is rude, I know. But I want to return to him quickly, before I chicken out. I shut the door behind me.

Phin's still sitting in his chair. He looks surprised to see me again, but not *that* surprised. Maybe he can read my mind, but I don't care, because I'm going to tell him myself what's on it.

"I stole your cat," I say.

Phin frowns. He points to a chair across the room. I pull it over and sit in front of him. I start talking, really fast.

"He was cold and scared and dirty and hungry when we found him, and he had a BB-gun pellet in his side," I say. "His name tag said *MUD*, which I thought was a terrible name for a cat. Actually, I still do, in my humble opinion, even though I guess I understand why you named him that."

"Slow. Down," says Phin, smiling.

I nod, take a deep breath, and continue.

"For a long, long time, I thought for sure he belonged to someone very cruel. My dad said I have an inventive mind, but I think I invented way too much this time. I threw away his name tag with your address on it. Nobody in the world knows I did that. Except you, now."

Phin is sitting very still, as if he's waiting for something.

"But I did keep the name tag with the diamond on it, just in case it was valuable," I say. "It wasn't, but of course you already know that. Anyway, we named him Zook because we love O'Leary's fried zucchini, and so does Zook. I want to tell you that I'm so sorry I stole him. I also want you to know he's had a happy life with us. A very, very happy life. And we've been happy because of Zook."

Phin's oxygen tank hisses quietly.

"You'd like O'Leary's, too. We can bring you one of their pizzas one day."

I stand up. Phin grabs my hand.

"I. Do. Understand," he says. "Maybe. It. Was. Meant. To. Be."

And that's when I decide to tell Phin everything, even though it seems as if he knows everything already. One thing's for sure: Phin understands what it's like when you don't get a chance to say good-bye. I sit down again.

"Do you have time to hear something else?" I ask.

"Lots," Phin says.

So I tell him the story going around and around in my head about visiting my dad in the hospital with Zook in that wicker basket covered up with the napkin with strawberries on it. About my dad calling him a furry taco and all of us laughing our heads off at that.

And then I tell Phin the part of the story I've never told out loud.

"I had to go to the bathroom. I couldn't help it. There was this teeny bathroom just two steps from Dad's bed. I didn't have to go far. I didn't take that long. When I got back into bed with him, my father was sleeping. I kissed his left earlobe, the one with the mole shaped like an avocado on it. His story ear, the one he always pulled before he told his stories. And my mother and I saw that he was lying very still. My father had died, you see. He was very, very sick. But I am so glad Zook was with him, keeping him warm and cozy all the way to the end, purring a song in his story ear. So glad. I wanted to tell you that, too."

Phin is still holding my hand. He takes my other one. He doesn't say anything for a few seconds. Then he says, "See? Meant. To. Be."

Phin's pauses make every word he says sound true and important. I'm thinking that Phin sounds like God talking, if God's a nice old African-American man with young eyes and an oxygen tank. I feel my sour, yellow-whopper lump start to melt inside of me. Tears fill up my eyes and my nose gets stuffed up, but I'm feeling good and I'm feeling sad all at once, like the blues.

"Tell. Your. Mother. Too," Phin says.

"OK," I say.

I get up and hug Phin, who smells like a eucalyptus tree. Maybe he's not God, but he's a great-grandfather figure now. Then I rub my eyes, because tears would ruin all that cheerfulness in the Home's corridors. Also, my mom would start asking nosy questions.

I'll tell her everything when I'm ready.

* 22 *

MY THEORY OF HAPPY-ENDING TIMES

According to my theory, happy-ending times feel like the happy endings in stories or movies or on TV, except you're having them in real life. Something nice happens and you start imagining cool background music playing, or people suddenly leaping up and dancing together, their arms and legs doing exactly the same thing in a coordinated way.

Happy-ending times happen all the time, but you have to be a good noticer, or they'll just pass you by. You can look back on your life and think, "Hey, that was one of them. I think." But it's so much better to catch them like a fastball, AT THE EXACT MOMENT they're happening. I've been catching more and more happy-ending times lately.

The time we all realized that Zook was Mud was a happy-ending time.

And the day I told Phin about my yellow whopper was another one, even though I was crying.

Another happy-ending time also involved Phin because of an idea I had. A really good one, in my humble opinion. I kept thinking about Phin being an indoor cat like Zook, all cooped up. I realized we didn't need to bring an O'Leary's pizza to Phin; instead, we'd bring Phin to O'Leary's! So we did. He came in his wheelchair with his oxygen tank and his guitar. Salvatore and Manic Moe hooked up two microphones, and Phin played guitar with Dylan. Dylan sang. You could almost see the musical notes dancing out the open window or squeezing under the crack in the door, just like in a cartoon. They waved their little note-tails at people passing by, who then followed the music into the store and ate some pizza.

"Hey, Phin, now you'll be a regular at this establishment!" I said.

Phin winked at me as he left, looking tired but pleased with himself. Dylan pushed him down the street to his truck, and the imaginary happy-ending orchestra played louder and louder as Phin and his wheelchair got smaller and smaller.

Some people look like they're having happy endings all the time—ever notice? My former first-grade teacher Miss Crackenhower has that look, with those big smiley white teeth of hers. I'll bet she hears music wherever she goes.

Another happy-ending time was when Freddy told me he knew how to read and would hardly need my help anymore.

"I keep getting fired from my jobs!" I said.

"Sorry about that," he said. "But I don't need any more rebuses. Those are for babies. I like sounding words out."

"OK, if you say so," I said. I winked at the imaginary video camera capturing the moment. Major happy-ending music started up. But then, after the imaginary commercial, there was the short funny part where I said I had to teach him a few more things. I pointed out that PH sounded like F, as in the word *phone*, and GH could, too, as in the word *enough*. And CH could sound like K, as in *school*, but had a different sound in *chug*.

"You're wrong," Fred said. "School is spelled S-K-O-O-L, like in Little Tots Playskool."

So we looked up *school* in the dictionary, and Freddy couldn't wait to tell his teacher about her big mistake.

If that were the ending of a show, they'd play a little doop-dee-doo tune right then. That means something funny has just happened, but tune in next time for more happy-ending shows.

Every time we give Zook his fluids, every time he leaps off that big brown chair looking healthy and beautiful, like all the promises of the world come true, has been a happy-ending time. Twice a day for thirty days makes sixty times I've heard music in my head.

Another happy-ending time happened in the Safeway supermarket and involved My Secret Love. I was in the frozen food section with my mother, and she was taking a long time deciding on ice cream flavors, which is one of the good things about having Dylan come for dinner: She serves dessert to make the meal last longer.

It was only out of the corner of my eye, but that's all I needed to recognize My Secret Love, passing by our aisle with a friend. My mom was still deep in thought. I quickly scooted down one aisle and up another. I strolled right toward My Secret Love going the other way. Unfortunately, he was talking to his friend as they were sharing a humongous bag of Cheez Doodles, and he didn't notice me.

So I zoomed down another aisle and raced around to the front of the store so I'd bump into him again as he and his friend emerged from aisle three. I coughed. He glanced at me, and I could tell he thought I looked familiar but really didn't recognize me. That's understandable, because I was wearing a new red T-shirt, and he's used to seeing me in a Raiders sweatshirt and eating pizza.

"You're . . . ?" he said, pointing his finger right at me.

"Oona!" I said. "From O'Leary's."

"Oh, right! Oona!" he said. "You're always hanging out there with that little kid."

I thought that was a great conversation starter on his part. "He's—" I started to say. I wanted to tell him that the little kid is my brother and his name is Freddy, and that Freddy and I, we're really good friends with the owners of the pizza establishment, and I'd be happy to get him some extra sides of zook, if he likes. And does he have any brothers or sisters?

But then his friend snickered and said, "Hey, Oona, Oona, sing me a tune-a!" He elbowed My Secret Love in the ribs. I didn't feel like singing, believe you me. I narrowed my eyes at the friend, a nincompoop Rowdy with an orange Cheez Doodly mustache. Maybe they weren't truly close friends.

But My Secret Love snickered, too, and elbowed back. And he had his own orange mustache, I noticed, but that wasn't the important thing, really.

The important thing was, the important thing IS, all of a sudden I knew everything you need to know about true love. And it's this:

1. True love does make you want to sing. For instance, *Baby, please don't go* or *Fiddle-i-fee*. It may even make you want to laugh. But not snicker.
2. True love shouldn't be so hard! True love should feel easy and meant to be, the way Dylan and my mom seem to feel about each other. And as easy as loving Zook. SO WHAT if Zook's a cat?
3. True love should make everyone feel happy because you are wonderful in the other person's eyes, and vice-versa, in a DOG IS GOD SPELLED BACKWARD sort of way.

I went back to my mother in the frozen food section. She'd chosen rum raisin and hadn't even realized I'd been gone. Or that I'd just had one of those happy-ending times, the kind of ending that comes at the end of a story when a character figures out something important about life. OK, I didn't feel exactly happy, but not exactly sad, either.

The other day I had a long conversation with Kiran. He is so smart. It was the deepest, most mature conversation I've had with a friend, ever. I imagine I will have conversations like that with a Real True Love one day.

Kiran said, "I don't like movies and books with happy endings. Real life isn't like that. Happy endings are juvenile."

Then he described his favorite movie, which is called *Casablanca.* It takes place during World War II and is considered the most popular and famous movie of all time, according to people online. It's very deep and doesn't have a very happy ending at all.

I said, "Well, real life isn't only about unhappy endings, either."

We went on and on about that, and finally we agreed to disagree. But then we realized that we actually agreed because real life has sometimes happy, sometimes unhappy, and sometimes bittersweet endings. But life keeps starting up again. Only stories end.

But then Kiran said, very softly and kindly, "Actually, things end in real life, too, if you know what I mean. Sorry to bring that up, Oona."

He meant what happened to my dad, etc., etc. I said I understood what he meant, and that he had a point. We didn't say anything else for a few minutes, but then Kiran said that death makes you appreciate all the happy times that have happened and that are going to happen in your life. I guess he's right.

But I don't want to think about that conversation anymore.

Because the truth is, it's actually been only fifty-nine times I've heard music in my head for Zook.

Tonight something is very wrong with him.

I wish I could invent a happy-ending room spray or something. I wish I had the power to make happy endings happen whenever I want to in real life, not just in stories.

23

PETS ROCK

Zook's been crying all night. It isn't a howling, but an every-now-and-then whimper, like a mouse's squeak. At some point Fred came down to my bunk. We lay in the dark on either side of Zook so he'd feel warm and safe.

"Hey," my mother whispers, waking me up. It seems as if I've been up all night, but I guess I did fall asleep. Fred wakes up, too. The three of us sit on my bed, looking down at Zook, whose eyes are open. I pat him and he purrs. Does he feel better? I wish he could tell us how he feels.

Dylan knocks on the half-open door. My mom tells him to come in, and Dylan bends down and takes Zook in his arms. Now Zook howls.

I cry out, "He was purring a second ago! We were petting him and he was purring happily. Please be gentle," I say.

"A cat's purr is a mysterious thing," Dylan says. "It means the cat is feeling something very strong, sometimes good, sometimes bad."

He carries Zook to the living room. Zook is still whimpering and purring as loud as an engine. We all follow. Dylan tries to give Zook his fluids. Zook pulls away and wails.

"He's too ill for this," Dylan says. "He's probably nauseated." He gently removes the needle and strokes Zook's back. He stands up, still cradling Zook. "He needs to go back to the vet. They'll decide what to do next."

"The vet? NO!" I shout. I stamp my foot.

"Oona . . . ," says my mother.

I know I'm acting like a baby. I can't help it. I am angry, but in a way I've never felt before, as if there are icy black stones rattling around inside my chest.

"Oona, he's very old," Dylan says. "It may be his time to go."

"He doesn't belong at the vet!" I say. "He belongs here, with our family." And I'm about to stamp my foot again, but I stop. "Time to go?" I say. "What's that supposed to mean?"

"He's suffering," Dylan says, looking quickly at my mother.

My mother puts her hand on Dylan's arm, giving it a short, hard squeeze. To my surprise, she glares at him. "Dylan, no more! I'll deal with the kids myself, I told you."

Dylan shrugs, and my mother gives him another hard look. Then she says, "Dylan and I will take him to the vet for an exam. Don't worry, kids."

Freddy and I get dressed, and then we wrap up Zook in my Raiders sweatshirt. We all pile into the car, me and Fred in the backseat, Zook between us. Zook's lying very still, crying every now and then. We pull up to the Little Tots Playskool. My mom takes Freddy inside, and Dylan and I wait in the car. Dylan is silent, looking out the window at the other cars going by. And I'm wishing with all my heart I were little like Freddy. Too little to know that grown-ups spell things wrong on purpose, for dumb, dumb, dumb reasons. Too little to understand what "time to go" really means.

My mom returns to the car and I say, "Don't take me to school. I'm going to the vet with you."

My mother turns to look at me. I make my mouth a hard straight line, the way she always does when nothing in the world will change her mind.

We drive to the Good Samaritan Veterinary Clinic, and I carry Zook inside. Evelyn has on a different pair of earrings this time, big, gold swaying hoops. She looks at us sorrowfully; we don't even have to say why we're here. An assistant whisks Zook to the back.

My mom and Dylan and I squeeze together on the waiting room couch. I realize I hate that scratched red leather couch with all of my heart. I look down at Dylan's hands, folded together on his lap, hands that look like they can fix things. "You said Zook would get better," I say. "You promised us."

Dylan nods. He reaches over and touches my shoulder. I shrug off his hand. "I did make that promise," he says. "I guess I shouldn't have. But Zook did have some pretty good days with us because of those fluids. Don't you think?"

Dylan's eyes are pleading with me to agree. But I don't want to agree. What I want to do is hurt someone. And I don't want to hurt my mom. I never want to hurt my mom again. So it has to be Dylan. Dylan, who can't make Zook better. And that's when those icy black stones inside of me turn into a couple of big black whoppers. The kind I've never told in my life, only heard about. The kind of whoppers meant to hurt.

"I think you were cruel to make a promise like that," I say. And then, "You know what? I wish we'd never even met you!"

"Oona," says my mom, flushing. She looks at Dylan. "She's upset. She doesn't really mean that."

"I do so mean it," I say.

Dylan looks at me.

I stare right back at him with narrowed eyes. I feel cruel. I don't even recognize myself.

Dylan bows his head. He looks down at his big boots, and his shoulders are kind of caved in. All of a sudden I wish I could take back that ugly black whopper, just reel it right in like a big old shoe on a fishhook.

But then I hear a cat's wail through the wall. I squeeze my mother's hand; we both know it's Zook.

The vet, Howard Fiske, DVM, comes out into the waiting room. "I'm sorry," he says. He looks as sad and serious as Evelyn. "He's suffering. I don't think we can do any more to help him." You can tell he really means it. He did his best.

Nobody says aloud that it's Zook's time to go. But of course it is.

My mother catches her breath and shakes her head. Dylan hugs her. "He has to be put down," he whispers. My mother stands up, and she's crying.

"Oona, wait here with Dylan," she says.

"No!" I say. I stand up, too.

"I told you, Oona. Wait here," my mother repeats.

"Terri, let her go in with you," Dylan says. "It will be OK."

"Dylan!" says my mom sharply.

"She'll be fine," says Dylan quietly. "Believe me."

I look at him and feel so grateful. "I'm going in," I say. "You can't stop me."

"Do you want me to go in, too?" Dylan asks.

My mom and Dylan are staring at each other. It seems as if a thousand seconds go by.

"No, don't," says my mother. "And I really don't know how long we'll be. Maybe Oona and I will want to be alone afterward."

"OK," says Dylan. "I won't wait for you."

I'm thinking now would be a good time for one of them to sing *Baby, please don't go*, but of course nobody feels much like singing.

Then everything happens very quickly.

My mother and I are in one of the examining rooms, our arms around each other, waiting. Soon Howard Fiske, DVM, and Dog/God come in, except today Dog/God is wearing a turquoise sweatshirt under a white coat. Her sweatshirt says PETS ROCK.

"You've met Isabel? Isabel's a veterinarian intern at Good Samaritan," says Howard Fiske, DVM.

My mom and I nod. My mom's still crying, and you know

what? So is Isabel. She's holding Zook in her arms, still wrapped in my Raiders sweatshirt. Zook is lying quietly, but his eyes are wide open and scared. A line of tubing is taped to one of his front legs, and I know it's for whatever they're going to give him to put him down.

"First, we're going to inject Zook with a sedative, so he'll feel very relaxed," Isabel says.

"I'd like to hold him," I say, and she carefully places him in my arms.

Isabel pulls a tissue from her pocket to wipe her nose, and I'm thinking she better get a hold of herself if she's going to be a vet. I myself am not crying. I am glad to be calm and mature for Zook and my mother. I suddenly feel Zook relax in my arms as they inject the sedative. I touch my lips to his cool, smooth ear with its brown tufts of hair sticking out.

"Good-bye, good-bye, good-bye," I whisper. Then I look right into Zook's eyes. He stares back at me. I can tell he feels brave and peaceful.

Howard Fiske, DVM, and Isabel are busy beside me, preparing the final injection. My mother puts her arm around me while they inject Zook once again.

Suddenly, Zook is very still.

"He's gone," Isabel says. She closes Zook's eyes. I lay him down on the examining table.

"We'll leave you alone with him," Howard Fiske, DVM, says. "Take as long as you like."

It wasn't like putting Zook "down," I'm thinking. It was like sending Zook up and away. Up and away and out of that tired old body filled with pain, which smells so familiar when I kiss it one last time. It smells like our house and my sweatshirt, and because of that, a little bit like my dad.

We go back to the waiting room. Dylan has gone. My mom signs some papers and Evelyn gives her Zook's collar and tags, which my mom puts into her purse.

"You'll receive Zook's ashes very soon," Evelyn says. "Then you can bury them. My own sweetie-pies are in my backyard garden."

I turn to my mom and we smile sadly at each other. A smile can have a whole conversation behind it—ever notice? And sometimes sad smiles are sadder than no smiles at all. We don't tell Evelyn that there's no backyard garden, just a balcony with a cactus plant and a grill on it, that our alley is sort of our backyard garden, that Dylan has a beautiful garden but I just sent him away with a big black whopper, and it looks like he and my mom had a big fight about something I don't totally understand. And anyway, it's only ashes. Our smiles say all that.

My mom cries a bit as we walk to Antoine's Bistro for lunch. I pat her shoulder. I've never eaten in a bistro before, which turns out to be a regular restaurant, actually. I order a hamburger and french fries and I request some vinegar on the side, for dipping my fries. You can tell it's a fancy establishment because the waiter doesn't say "VINEGAR?" like a lot of waiters do in other restaurants. My mother orders fish. She has a glass of wine and I have orange juice, but my juice is in a wine goblet, like hers. I feel mature, like I'm on a date or something, except, of course, I'm with my mom.

We go over to Gramma Dee's to get Fred. She'd left work early to pick him up at preschool.

"I didn't tell him," Gramma Dee whispers.

That night Fred and I are in our pj's, and Fred's on the floor making towers with his LEGOs. LEGOs are very relaxing things. Everything fits and clicks together so nicely. I sit down on the floor and help him.

My mom's on my bed, fiddling with a button on her blouse. She takes a deep breath and says, "I have to tell you something sad, Freddy. Zook died today."

Freddy's constructing a very tall tower. One more LEGO and it'll fall down. He looks up at me, frowning. I nod my head. "Oh," he says. Then he adds that last LEGO, and sure enough, the tower topples over. And Fred starts stacking it all up again.

"Fred, did you understand what I've just told you?" asks my mother.

"Of course I did! I'm not a baby," Fred says. "But Zook's coming back. When do you think that will be?"

My mother looks startled. She slides off the bed onto the floor. "What do you mean, honey? I just told you, Zook has died."

"Yes, but not really, right, Oona? Oona told me cats have nine lives. Other people said the same thing. Zook's only lived five of them, and he has four more lives to go." Fred holds up all his fingers, hiding the thumb on his right hand. He wriggles the fingers and thumb on his left hand, as he calls out the names for Zook's five lives. "Miraculo! Jewel! Beau! Mud! Zook!" Then he wriggles the four fingers of his right hand. "See? Four more to go. So when's he coming back?"

"Why did you tell him that, Oona?" my mother asks.

I examine the yellow daisy pattern on my pajama bottoms. I can't look at her. I am so ashamed of my whoppers. "I wanted to make Freddy feel better. So I told him some stories about Zook's other lives. And, yes, I did promise that Zook had four more left." I glance at my brother. "Freddy, I'm so sorry. Actually, cats have only one life to live."

Fred still has his hands up. He slowly puts them down. "Only one?" he asks.

"Only one," I say. "We all do. You're a big boy now. You can read. And now you know this very deep, mature, important thing about all living things."

And right then is when I put my head on my mother's shoulder and bawl like a baby. It has been such a hard, hard day.

I cry for Zook.

I cry for my father.

I cry for all those extra lives nobody gets to live.

I try to stop crying, being the older sister and all that. I don't want to scare my brother. So I think about Kiran's deep, mature idea about death making us appreciate the wonderful things about life. All those happy, happy happy-ending times. That helps a little. After a while, I start feeling empty inside. All those icy black stones have melted and turned into the fluids pouring out of me.

Except there's one stone left. A big yellow one. So I tell my mother how I threw away Zook's old name tag when he used to be called Mud, and how I spied on Dylan when he used to be the Villain. I tell her that I'd apologized to Phin that day at the Home, and that Phin gave me some advice: to tell her the truth. I keep my face on my mother's shoulder. I don't want to see the angry look on her face, or what would be even worse, the sad one.

But my mother lifts my head from her shoulder, and she's smiling. With her eyes, too, except there are tears in them. "You mean you kept those secrets inside you all this time? That must have been so hard, my darling."

"It was," I say. I look over at Fred, who's just sitting there, staring down at his LEGOs.

My mother puts one arm around each of us. "The thing is," she says, "I think the Great Rebus-Maker and Whopper-Teller would have told all the same whoppers."

"Really?" I say.

"Oh, yes," says my mother. "There's so much of him in both of you. And that sure helps me get through the night to greet the day. Lives continue on in lots and lots of ways."

24

Life Number Five

ZOOK

Everyone has been very understanding these past few weeks. Mr. Fry sent a beautiful scalloped, gold-trimmed sympathy card through snail mail.

Riya composed a poem and e-mailed it to me the other day.

It doesn't matter whether the owner or the pet is the boss;
When your pet dies, it's still a great loss.

Kiran wrote, *My sincerest condolenses. R.I.P., ZOOK!*

I've also received e-mails and notes and cards from kids in my class who have suffered the loss of a pet. Even from Rowdies.

Heard what happened. I thought I would never stop thinking about my beagle, Phil, every single minute, wrote Leo. *But I feel better now.* He put the note on my desk at school.

Zook's ashes were delivered by UPS. We had to sign for them. They came in a plastic bag stuffed into a pretty tin can with dogs and cats painted all over it. We keep the tin can on our bookshelf until we can decide what to do with the ashes. Nobody can agree.

Gramma Dee suggested burying them in Soma's yard, but Zook was our pet, not Soma's. Fred wants to leave them in the box on the shelf. I agree. I do like looking at it from time to time. It's only a box of ashes, but it gets me thinking good thoughts, although it's hard to imagine Zook resting in peace in that box.

"How about we go to the beach today and scatter Zook's ashes over the waves?" my mother asks.

"That doesn't make sense," I say. "Zook hated getting wet."

My mom laughs. "That doesn't make sense, either," she says. "Anyway, it's such a lovely Saturday. We should do something outdoors."

My mother is ironing and folding her fancy napkins. She puts them in the special kitchen drawer with the fancy tablecloths and coasters and other things we hardly use. We're back to paper napkins again. Dylan hasn't come around for dinner in a while, or even to take my mom out for coffee.

"Cloth napkins are much better for the environment, by the way," I tell her.

"Who's to say? Washing them uses too much water. And I've tried, but I just can't get all the stains out," my mother says.

They're not big stains, just enough to tell whose napkin is whose. My stains are raspberry juice and a splotch of mustard. Mom's is a wine stain and a squiggle of gravy. Dylan's is spaghetti sauce, and Fred's is practically everything. I ask my mom if the napkins remind her of Dylan and that's why she's not using them anymore.

"Oh, I don't know," she says. She smiles a big cheery smile. "It's all for the best, really. We decided everything happened much too fast! And Dylan's going on another long bike trip soon." My mother keeps that big smile on her face like news announcers on TV sometimes do, even when they're reporting murders and car accidents.

"But you were right," my mother continues. "Dylan should never have made that promise about Zook getting well."

"Zook had some really good days with us because of those fluids," I say. What I don't say is, if it was all for the best, how come everyone seemed happier when Dylan was around?

"Anyway, Dylan said we all needed lots more time to heal," says my mother. With her foot, she pushes the drawer of napkins closed, and then she turns toward the kitchen window. "Look at this glorious day! Why don't the three of us have lunch in the park? Or go for a bike ride? Oona, come on, shut down the computer! I'll go find Fred."

I turn back to the computer. *Thank you for your kind words, Amanda,* I write. *And sorry for the loss of your hamster, Scratchy.*

My mother comes back into the kitchen. "I can't find Fred anywhere," she says.

"He was just here a little while ago," I say. In my mind, Freddy's a quick flash of blue shorts and the sound of the fridge opening and closing.

By the way, Amanda, why do you prefer hamsters over guinea pigs and gerbils? What's the difference, anyway?

I delete that last question because it doesn't sound very sympathetic. I'll do my own research, or ask Amanda in person sometime.

The bathroom door slams. I can hear my mom running from room to room. She opens the front door and shouts for

Fred in the hallway. Then she's back in the kitchen, her face almost as pale as our walls.

"Oona, he's not here," she says.

I stand up so quickly, my chair falls over. My mom grabs her purse and phone. We don't even bother with the elevator, racing down the stairs. No sign of him up or down the block. Luckily, my mom got a spot for the car right in front of the building, so we get right in and she zooms over to Dylan's. I jump out of the car and ring his doorbell. No answer. I press the bell so hard, my finger hurts. I can hear the ring echoing inside. I start pounding on the door. My mother runs to the backyard.

Please please please, both of you be here!

My mom races out front again, breathing hard. "No one's there. No answer on Dylan's cell, either," she says.

She phones Gramma Dee. She phones Soma. She phones O'Leary's. She phones and sends texts to friend after friend after friend, her fingers flying over the teeny keyboard.

We drive through the neighborhood, me looking out the window to the north, my mom to the south.

"I'm going to drop you off at our building in case he comes back," says my mother. We are both crying. "Wait right there. I'll continue driving around. If I don't see him soon, I'm calling the police."

I stand in front of our building. People hurry by, carrying bags filled with flowers from the farmer's market, listening to music on their iPods, eating ice cream. It seems as if everyone is smiling, because that's what sunshine makes you do. No one knows that something terrible has happened in our family. Freddy has disappeared.

Today is Saturday, sunny and warm. The air is still and clear, and you can hear the birds over the traffic noise, and smell the eucalyptus tree over the traffic smells. Just like that other Saturday. Freddy knows every detail of the story, even though he doesn't really remember that day, the day we found Zook. But he thinks he does, because he's heard about it so many times.

I run down the driveway to the back of our building. The catmint and yellow yarrow that my father and I planted are growing tall in the cracked concrete. I don't see Fred, but I know he's been here. The hose is stretched across the alley. Water is dripping from one of the blue pots, the one with the rosemary that Fred and Dylan planted together.

Then I see Freddy's foot. There he is in the shade of the

camellia tree, hunched up against the fence across from the ELVIS LIVES sign on the alley wall.

I kneel down.

"Hey," I say.

Freddy's brought a ziplock bag filled with bunny-shaped crackers, a half-eaten nectarine, and a large chunk of sourdough bread. He plans to be sitting there for a while.

"What're you doing here?" I ask, as if I don't know.

"Waiting," he says. "For Zook."

"Zook died, Freddy," I say.

"Well, he's coming back. Cats have hundreds and hundreds of lives. You don't know everything."

I sigh. "OK. I don't know everything. But we may have to wait a long time."

Fred looks at me, then looks away. "Who cares? I'll be here."

"Mom's really spooked, Fred," I say.

"No she's not," says Fred. "She knows where I am. Doesn't she?"

I forgot. Five-year-olds think moms can read minds.

"No, she doesn't know where you are," I say.

Fred's face kind of crumples up. He's torn between Mom and Zook now.

I sit down and put my arm around him. I feel like I have

an important job to do, the most important job I've ever had: making Fred happy again and bringing him home. I hear Bleet the goat rustling in the grass on the other side of the fence. I lean against the fence as if I have all the time in the world to wait for Zook with my brother.

"Are you thirsty?" I ask. "It's hot, even under this branch. Mom has cold apricot nectar in the refrigerator."

"I'm not thirsty. I drank from the hose when I watered my plant."

"Your rosemary's looking really good," I say.

He glances over at the pot. "I hadn't watered it for a long time."

"Rosemary doesn't need much water," I say. "It's drought-tolerant, like Dylan said. Hey, how about we plant more herbs in the other pots, and maybe some lavender and geraniums? Even a giant pickapoo plant! Bring some lawn chairs back here, too. We could have our own private, beautiful back garden, just like we used to have when Dad was with us. Let's buy the plants today."

"What's a pickapoo plant, anyway?"

"I made that up. Actually, Dad did. It's anything you want it to be, I guess. I'm trying to get you to smile."

Fred doesn't smile.

And then comes the question I knew he would ask, sooner or later. "Dylan's coming back, too, right?" He asks it quickly, like he doesn't really want an answer.

"I don't know," I say.

I feel sad that Dylan is Freddy's father figure. Freddy doesn't really remember our dad that well. But maybe if I keep telling stories about Dad, he'll think he does, especially if I put Zook in those stories.

I reach for a bunny cracker.

"Hey, do you remember the night Dad heard a rattling noise from the kitchen and called the cops? And the cops showed up and it was only Zook with his head stuck in an empty vegetable soup can? And they arrested him?"

Fred's eyes grow big. "Dad?"

"No, Zook. They put pawcuffs on him and took him downtown for questioning."

"You're being silly."

"Dad put up two bags of kitty litter for Zook's bail."

I get a small smile out of Freddy for that one. I'll take it.

"And do you remember how Dad cut out some magazine pictures and pasted them on the wall, low down, so Zook could enjoy his own private art gallery?"

"I think I do," Fred says. He's wrinkling up his forehead, and you can tell he's trying very hard to remember.

We take turns dipping into the bag of bunny crackers. Fred's appetite has been good these past few weeks. That's why we weren't that worried about him. We should have been. My heart hurts when I look at my brother, small and lonely, with that Sad Fred Look.

"Listen, who says Zook will show up again in the same place we found him?" I ask. "Miraculo and Jewel and Beau and Mud ended up in all sorts of places, in all kinds of weather. And it doesn't have to be a Saturday. He could come back any day of the week."

BINGO! Fred gives me a quick, happy look, a look which zings me with happiness, too. "You're right!" he says.

I'm thinking there must be a special color for a whopper you really, really want to believe, and sometimes you do. You imagine that if you tell it, even to yourself, maybe it will come true. A whopper about living things having lots of lives, for instance. Or a whopper about someone being a villain so you can keep his sweet, singing cat. Or a promise like the one Dylan made, that Zook would get well.

It's the color of a wish, if a wish had a color. Maybe it's a color that's only seen in outer space. Or maybe it's multicolored, wrapped up like a birthday gift.

"And you know what else? I think there's a chance Dylan will come back," I say. "A really, really good chance he'll come back."

Fred scrambles to his feet. "Let's go tell Mom," he says.

25

A DELIVERY

We are all at O'Leary's—me, Freddy, Mom, and Gramma Dee. Mario and Maria are sitting at the long table, eating with us, too. I like that. My Secret Used-to-Be-Probably-Never-Was-True Love is at a corner table with his own family. Maybe he notices that the owners are sitting with us, like we're celebrities or something. I hope he'll ask me how I know the owners, and then I can tell him coolly that, oh, we're all old, old friends, and also, Fred and I are employees of the establishment. Well, pizza interns of the establishment. The whole staff is teaching us pizza know-how.

In fact, the pizza we're all digging into is one that Freddy and I helped make. It's pretty good. Manic Moe gave me some tips for stretching the dough, except I'm not good at tossing the dough into the air and catching it, like he does. Manic Moe says that part will come with experience. Freddy himself swirled on the sauce. We also put the herbs and vegetables on top—zucchini blossoms and tomato slices and green peppers and basil and rosemary.

The rosemary is Fred's. The rest of the vegetables and herbs are Dylan's. Nobody at our table mentions that. Maria told me that Dylan gets up at the crack of dawn and delivers it all, still wet with dew. I guess he hasn't started his long bike trip yet. We ourselves haven't seen him in almost three weeks.

"Fabulous," says Gramma Dee. "Best pizza I've ever had at O'Leary's."

"Not bad for trainees," says my mother. She has sauce on the corners of her mouth. It's a very juicy pizza.

Mario glances quickly at his watch. Then he looks up as the bell on the door tinkles. "Just in time," he says. "It's our delivery."

Well, it's Dylan who's making that delivery, carrying a wicker basket, even though it's six P.M. and not the crack of dawn. He looks at me, then at Freddy, who runs to him and hugs his legs.

"I knew it!" Freddy shouts. "I knew you'd come back!"

Dylan picks him up with one arm and comes over to where we're all sitting. He gently places the wicker basket on the table, and we all lean over to see what's in it.

It's not vegetables and herbs. It's an orange-and-white kitten.

"Zook!" Freddy says. "It's Zook!"

Dylan lifts the kitten from the basket and gives it to Fred. The kitten splays its limbs, then suddenly relaxes its body against Freddy's shoulder.

"Of course, he isn't Zook anymore," Freddy says. "He's Elvis, now."

"Elvis is a girl," Dylan says.

"So what?" says Freddy.

I quickly count Elvis's toes. Eighteen, not twenty-six. But I do notice that her eyes are a beautiful blue, like blue suede shoes, and when I squint I can see a white map of California on her belly.

Dylan hasn't looked at my mother yet, but then he does, and my mom is crying tears of joy, as beautiful as diamonds. He sits down beside her and they hug, and she gets tomato sauce on his shirt. They look like people in love at the end of a movie, an ending that's both happy and sad, like the blues.

Of course, it's not the end of anything. But I will still tell this story to Baby Hope of the World, who, in my humble opinion, they'll probably have.

I really think Dylan would have come back even if I hadn't secretly texted PLEASE DON'T GO, WE LOVE YOU SO, FROM OONA on my mom's cell. Maybe Mario told him to come back, too.

I really think Dylan came back to us because of true love. And also because Freddy and I made that wish on Zook's fake diamond.

Oh, Zook. Thank you for everything.

* 26 *

THE THEORY OF STORY-MAKING FROM OONA AND THE GREAT REBUS-MAKER AND WHOPPER-TELLER

1. Stories are whoppers, but in a good way.
2. If a story is going around and around in your head, that gets annoying—ever notice? So tell it to someone. Or write it down.
3. You make a story yours by taking pieces of your world and putting them in your story to make a whole other world. These pieces are called details.
4. A story doesn't have to be true, but it does have to be real. That makes it truly a story. So even if it's a fantasy, try to make the whopper-getter believe it could really happen. That's where details help.
5. The more you tell or write your story, the more you want to add some details to it. That's OK. Each time you complete

a new version of your story, that's called a draft. Details are like jigsaw puzzle pieces, helping your drafts become whole.

6. If the ending fits, use it. Even if you say "To be continued" because you're having so much fun with the story, there still has to be some sort of ending. It doesn't even have to be a totally happy ending. It could be happy and sad at the same time.
7. Your story will make you, the whopper-teller, feel good when you tell it or write it.
8. Your story will make the whopper-getter feel good, especially if your puzzle pieces are pieces of that person's puzzle, too.

Acknowledgments

Thank you, Eric Silverberg, for making me aware of the work of Barrel of Monkeys (barrelofmonkeys.org). BOM inspires kids in public schools to write their stories, which this wonderful Chicago theater troupe then performs. "The kids become stars and the world is saved. The End."

And thank you, Rupa Basu, for broadening our lives in so many ways. And Sarah Jackson, for your practical wisdom, and Michael Silverberg, for your loving support, always. Thank you, Karen Gaiger and Jim Gaiger for all the laughs. And Jackee Berner and Marjan Shomali for your beautiful writing spaces. And thank you, Gerry Nelson, for the subcutaneous fluids, and much, much more. A big thank-you to my editor, Maggie Lehrman, and the rest of the Abrams team, and also to my agent, Erin Murphy, for those encouraging shout-outs. Thanks to Chris Buzelli for his wonderful cover and Robyn Ng for the interior artwork.

And thank you to my grandchildren for their stories, too.

I am grateful for the assistance of everyone at Montclair Veterinary Hospital, Oakland, California, especially Dr. Gary Richter, who knows that Howard Fiske, DVM, is a figment of my imagination.

And to all my pets, past and present, especially our cat Mitzi, working on her umpteenth life despite the BB-gun pellet—thank you for everything.

About the Author

JOANNE ROCKLIN is the critically acclaimed author of several books, including *One Day and One Amazing Morning on Orange Street*, which earned starred reviews and which *School Library Journal* called "sweet and tart and sure to satisfy." She's also the author of *Strudel Stories*, which was a *School Library Journal* Best Book of the Year and an American Library Association Notable Book, and *For YOUR Eyes Only!*, which was a *School Library Journal* Best Book and a Bank Street Best Book. She lives in Oakland, California.

This book was designed by Maria T. Middleton. The text is set in 13-point FF Atma Serif, a modern typeface that incorporates transitional elements similar to those found in Baskerville. FF Atma Serif was designed by Alan Dague-Greene in 2001 for the FontFont type foundry. The interior illustrations were drawn by Robyn Ng.

This book was printed and bound by R.R. Donnelley in Crawfordsville, Indiana. Its production was overseen by Erin Vandeveer.